ZACH KRYTON
THRILLER

POSEIDON

JOSH
FRANCIS

Poseidon – The Zach Kryton Introductory Series Book 2

This is the sequel to Pegasus – it is recommended you read it first

WARNING: some obscene language

Copyright 2020

Josh Francis

ISBN: 978-0-6487025-1-1 (paperback)

Published by Red Diamond
www.red-diamond.com.au

Sign up to the reader's group

This story is fictional!

Cover media by Onur Aksoy – Great work Onur!
www.onegraphica.com

Also By Josh Francis

Pegasus – The Zach Kryton Introductory Series (Book 1).

Poseidon – The Zach Kryton Introductory Series (Book 2).

Phoenix – The Zach Kryton Introductory Series (Book 3).

Battle Rhythm – The military-inspired personal planning, discipline and motivation guide (The Camouflage Series Book 1).

Centre of Gravity – The principles soldiers use to think, act and achieve success (The Camouflage Series Book 2).

Under the Pump – Anecdotes of a service station operator.

Follow Us

You can find other publications and join our conversations on social media. This will keep you up to date with upcoming books and allow you to share ideas. Feel free to contribute!

INSTAGRAM

FACEBOOK

AMAZON

Please leave an honest review on Amazon. This helps to tailor and improve the content of what we produce.

Contents

1

Situation Room – White House
Washington DC
0730 local

The packed room stood to attention as President Jack Lang walked in to receive the morning intelligence update.

"Be seated, y'all," he said firmly in his distinctive southern drawl as he took a seat at the head of the table, not making eye contact with any of them but instead looking at the notes in his hand.

He quickly rifled through the notes while the Secretary of State, Bradley Kingston, looked over his shoulder.

They conferred quietly while the room sat in silence.

The Secretary took his seat as the President looked over to the woman sitting at the far corner of the table.

"Anna," he said simply to the Director of the Central Intelligence Agency, Anna Dawn, indicating that he wanted her to talk.

"Good Morning, Mister President. I'll defer to the Chairman to present this morning's brief," she informed the President, before looking over to her right at the naval officer standing next to a set of television screens with maps displayed on them.

The President nodded, then looked up at the screens mounted on the wall at the end of the table.

"What have you got, Admiral?"

Admiral William Pike took in a deep breath before speaking. As Chairman of the Joint Chiefs of Staff, he was used to briefing the President and senior government officials on a regular basis.

Today's brief was different, though. They were at the back end of several days of intense intelligence collection and analysis, and the agencies were presenting their findings.

"Mister President, we can now confirm that the Chinese Navy has deployed the majority of its South Sea Fleet into the South China Sea."

The President looked intensely at the screens before him, which superimposed the known positions of Chinese military assets over a map of the South China Sea.

"Go on," he said.

"We are tracking seven destroyers, nine frigates, the carrier *Liaoning*, as well as about two dozen corvettes and submarines as having deployed rapidly into the area in the past five days," the Chairman continued.

"Jesus, that was quick," muttered the Secretary softly.

"Additionally, approximately one-hundred fighter aircraft and three brigades of the PLA, constituting approximately seven-thousand soldiers, have also been deployed," added the Chairman, referring to the Peoples Liberation Army – the titular name given to all of the Chinese military.

Admiral Pike paused for a moment to allow the President to digest the numbers. President Lang was well regarded by the senior members of the national intelligence community as well as the military leadership who now sat at the table with him. He listened, observed, and always allowed them to give their opinions and expertise before making a decision.

He knew the role of each agency and department intimately – both their capabilities and their limitations.

He had no time for fools or bullshit, and they knew it.

"John, other military movements?" he asked the Director of the National Security Agency, General John Blake of the U.S. Army.

"Sir, we are following an intense amount of chatter that indicates both the Chinese Northern and Eastern Fleets are also preparing to deploy, and their coastal defence units have been placed on high alert," briefed the NSA Director.

President Lang stood up and walked over to the screens for a closer look at the maps. He noted the blue dots and circles which indicated the positions of U.S. forces.

"Tell me about our forces in the area," he said looking at the Chairman before returning to his seat.

"Sir, the Pacific Fleet, like all U.S. military forces, was placed on alert at your order after the incident in Timor-Leste last week. The Seventh Fleet is currently deployed, almost in full, and is currently loitering in the Philippine Sea. Led by the carrier *Ronald Reagan*, they can be in the South China Sea within forty-eight hours."

The Chairman scrolled across the electronic screen and used a small wooden pointer to indicate the area he was talking about, showing the massive U.S. fleet postured to the east of the Chinese South Sea Fleet.

"The remaining elements are postured in the East China Sea, near South Korea. The Third Fleet is preparing and can deploy an additional two carrier battle groups within twenty-four hours out of San Diego on your order, sir."

The President continued to look at the screen closely, taking mental notes. He nodded slowly.

"Thank you, Admiral," he said as the Chairman took a seat at the table.

He leaned back into his leather chair and ran his hands through his thinning hair. He looked to his Secretary of State.

"Brad, what are our allies doing?"

Secretary Kingston sat forward in his own chair and looked over some notes.

"Mister President, as you can imagine the nations in the region are nervous."

The President listened carefully, looking between the maps on the screen and the other leaders at the table.

The Secretary continued briefing.

"The South Koreans are focusing on North Korean activity, which is virtually nil at this point. Japan, Vietnam, The Philippines – they're all worried and have placed their own militaries on high alert. I've been in contact with all of their ambassadors and they're wondering what our response will be."

The President scanned the room. It was obvious many at the table had the same question. He could sense their desire for action. However, the President was a rational man. He wouldn't drop bombs without evidence or proof.

"Okay, that's the regional picture. What's the media saying?"

Secretary Kingston answered.

"The media narrative remains that this was a Chinese sponsored attack, meant as a precursor to further expansion into the South China Sea, and possibly even wider afield."

"Based on what?" asked President Lang.

"Australian media picked up Timorese social media posts which had images of the Chinese men detained in Dili. This was quickly linked to Timorese media reporting of the murder of a security guard at Dili

Harbour. U.S. press agencies picked it up and have run with it, so have most international outlets," said the Secretary. "They're saying it was a covert effort to initiate conflict, which would justify Chinese military deployments in order to 'protect' their assets in the region."

The President rolled his eyes. He never could understand how some news agencies could quickly jump to conclusions. Then again, his own intelligence agencies were struggling to find verifiable answers, and he appreciated the public desire to get answers quickly.

"What more do we know about the attack on Air Force One, Anna?" he said, now looking at the CIA Director, seeking to gain a better understanding of the events that had led them to the situation.

"Well, sir, we think that it's possible that a Chinese submarine offloaded a small team of operatives into Timor-Leste in order to carry out the attack on Air Force One, having synchronised the attack with your flight to Jakarta," she commenced.

"This flight was aborted once the cyber-attack occurred, and your plane was almost shot down using stolen American Stinger missiles."

"I'm aware of that part," said President Lang drolly.

His intense gaze at Admiral Pike left the Chairman in no doubt about the Commander-in-Chief's dissatisfaction that American ordnance had not only been stolen, but had also been used against them.

"Where is that Chinese submarine now? Are we tracking it?" asked the President.

"Naval intelligence is struggling to locate it, sir. The theory about the covert infiltration, and it's still only a theory, is based on the fact we were tracking multiple Chinese submarines in the region, and one disappeared in that area in the days preceding the attack," said the Admiral.

"How do we lose a submarine?" asked the President.

"Sir, we weren't tracking it with one of our submarines, but rather with the sonar and communications networks we have covering the region. Sometimes they get through, especially the older diesel-electric type submarines."

The President sighed.

"It happens. It's a big ocean," said Secretary Kingston in support of the Admiral.

"Okay. What about the other surrounding facts that may tell us who was behind this?" the President asked.

"That is what we hope to find out by this afternoon from our interrogations," said the CIA Director. "The Australians don't know any more than us, and their man is leading the interrogation."

"The one who stopped the attack?" asked the President.

"Yes, sir," she replied.

Having a non-U.S. operative take the lead in the interrogation of a potential terrorist suspect, especially one who had attempted to assassinate the President, was highly unprecedented.

However, essentially outsourcing interrogation to a third party gave the CIA one thing they hadn't had in the post-Iraq and Afghanistan senate committee hearings into breaches of detainee rights.

Plausible deniability.

Even though they had removed some of the less palatable methods from their toolbox with the induction of the recently appointed Director, the CIA was wary to not allow itself to be accused of such activities again.

"Sir," continued Director Dawn, "we're currently interrogating one of the suspects at a Black Site in the South Pacific. We expect initial reports within the next few hours. Unfortunately, the few days it took us to gain custody of the Persian suspect from the Timorese authorities has set us back in getting a full intelligence picture."

"Persian?" queried the President.

The CIA Director nodded to an aide sitting in the corner, who pressed a few buttons on a laptop, bringing onto the screen the picture of the Persian man who had attempted to blow Air Force One out of the sky less than a week earlier.

So that's the little prick, President Lang thought to himself.

He looked at Secretary Kingston.

"Iranian involvement?"

Secretary Kingston looked over at the NSA Director, seeking his knowledge.

"Well, there's a lot of chatter from the region praising the attack, but nothing to suggest or indicate their involvement at this time," briefed the NSA Director.

"Go on, Anna," said the President.

"The Chinese government is flatly denying any involvement, even going to the point of denouncing it openly in the public sphere. The Australians have detained two Chinese nationals involved in the attack, and are questioning them in Dili. We hope to gain some more fidelity through these two men."

"Do we know *how* the systems on Air Force One failed?" asked the President, looking at Director Blake.

"Sir, we know that somehow the navigation and communication systems were susceptible to a cyber-attack which killed off those systems mid-flight. We've been able to recover some data and we now know that the origin of the attack was in the South China Sea."

"*Where* exactly?" asked the President, pushing for more detail.

The Director looked flabbergasted – and tired.

They all were.

He didn't have all the answers yet, and he knew that the President, indeed the American people, wanted them.

"We just don't know yet, Mister President. There is so much data to go through. It may take us a few days. We've got the best people on this. We're desperately trying to ascertain how our systems were able to be penetrated mid-flight."

President Lang raised his hand up empathetically. He knew they were all under intense pressure.

He looked at the screen for a moment, then again around the room.

"In all honesty. Was this a state-sponsored attack, or terrorism?" he asked openly.

No one gave an immediate answer.

Intelligence agencies were used to giving assessments based on very little information, but the fact remained that after almost a week since the President was almost blown out of the sky over Dili, they still didn't have a complete picture.

And they knew that a wrong assessment could lead to decisions that had fatal consequences that would come back to bite them.

The NSA Director shuffled in his chair as if he was about to speak. This caught the President's attention.

"John. Your thoughts," President Lang said.

"Sir, I'd like to see what Anna's team can extract from the suspect, but from what we're hearing from the Chinese chatter, they appear very confused themselves."

"Confused?" asked Secretary Kingston.

"Yes. Like they don't know what's going on and are asking many of the same questions we are. Until we know for sure it was actually the Chinese, I don't think we should do anything to provoke them. The whole region could go up in flames if we react too hastily," added the Director.

"Their military deployments, while rapid, do currently appear defensive in nature. Most of their naval assets have taken positions surrounding their military establishments in the South China Sea," added the Chairman.

"If we don't act now, we'll be on the back foot, and our allies will think we've abandoned them if the Chinese take an opportunity to expand into other areas in the region," argued Secretary Kingston.

A small murmur erupted in the room as the leaders started discussing amongst themselves.

Some disagreed with the Chairman, arguing that it was the beginning of Chinese expansion. Others urged caution.

President Lang let them chat.

He thought for a moment to himself.

Who had organised the attack?

Where in the South China Sea had it been conducted from?

What was the Chinese intent?

So many questions still outstanding.

He then sat upright in his chair to address the audience and made some more notes in his folder.

"Admiral Pike, hold the Third Fleet in place for now, and keep the Seventh Fleet in place out of the area."

"Yes, sir," replied the Chairman.

"But I want some response options for the moment we know for sure if it was them."

The Admiral nodded that he understood.

"There are too many information gaps. We need more intelligence. We need it now. Anna, do what you need to do, I want a full brief back here at 1700 hours," he said authoritatively.

"Because at midnight, if nothing's changed, I'm sending the Seventh Fleet into the South China Sea."

The room stood to attention as the President rose from his chair to leave.

"The Secretary here and I are pretty thick-skinned, so we won't take it all too personally. But I'd sure like to know who tried to light up our asses last week," he said firmly in a typically Southern way.

He looked over to the side of the room where a small television was showing round-the-clock coverage of the evolving situation.

"And so do the American people."

2

The wailing sound of a screaming baby filled the hot, cavernous room. A small lamp in the corner provided the slightest bit of illumination. A heater blasted warm air throughout the otherwise cold, darkened void.

Although the noise was being blasted out of several speakers, it sounded real enough.

A human in pain.

A mind-numbing noise.

In the middle of the room, hands and feet bound and sitting in the most uncomfortable position, sat the Persian man who had failed to shoot Air Force One out of the sky less than a week earlier.

His head was aching from the deliberately loud shrill noise that felt like it was penetrating every part of his body, to the point it made him feel like his bones were rattling.

He was breathing heavily. Thick sweat was forming beads all over his near-naked body. He tried to turn his head, but there was no escaping the noise or the heat.

Across the other side of the room was a mirror embedded into the wall. Standing behind it and observing the pitiful scene through the one-way mirror was Zach Kryton.

He grasped a mug in his hand and stood watching. The noise of the screaming baby was muffled by the insulation of the observation room.

This was his interrogation, and he would control its pace and intensity.

But he could empathise with what the Persian was being put through.

Having the person who actually captured the detainee lead the interrogation meant that an authoritative dynamic had already been established between the two. Most interrogations are battles of will. The interrogator trying to establish dominance; the detainee trying to hold out and not be broken. In this instance, though, Kryton had already won the first part.

He'd already proven dominance by having ensured that the Stinger missile didn't hit Air Force One, and then again by having captured the Persian – standing over his prey in Dili with a pistol pointed at his head.

Life or death at the Australian's discretion.

The task now was to break the pitiful man down and get him to want to talk.

"How's it looking?"

Kryton turned slightly to find U.S. Navy SEAL Clay Dalton standing next to him, also looking into the interrogation room.

His arm and upper chest were still bandaged from the gunshot wound he had received during the chase of the truck in Dili.

"I'll give him another twenty to thirty minutes," replied Kryton.

Dalton nodded.

Kryton had been interrogating the Persian for a little over twenty-four hours.

The mix of questioning, being placed in uncomfortable positions and loud uninterrupted noise was designed to throw the detainee off balance.

To make him want to answer Kryton's questions in order to stop what he was being put through.

"What have you learned?" asked Dalton.

"His name is Behrouz Bachar," said Kryton. "Not much else. He tried to be all tough when he got here, so I've been trying to soften him up a bit."

"Is the baby noise an Australian thing?" asked the SEAL.

Kryton grinned slightly. Not in pleasure from putting the Persian through the interrogation, but in memory from his own experiences undergoing interrogation training back in Australia.

"We've found it's more disturbing that other white noise."

"How so?" asked Dalton.

"It plays to human emotion. Most people are naturally wired to want to help someone in pain, especially children," Kryton said.

"Even terrorists?" asked Dalton.

"Well, it can help us get an idea of their character, and whether it presses their buttons or not. And if that doesn't press any buttons, then it's just fucking annoying having that in your head for hours on end," Kryton said as he looked at Dalton matter-of-factly.

Dalton smiled slightly.

"When I did my training, the PSYOPS guys just played music at one million decibels. I can't hear a Wiggles song anymore without wanting to punch someone," observed Dalton humorously, recalling the torture inflicted by the U.S. Army Psychological Operations Team during his own SEAL training.

Kryton chuckled.

Their conversation was interrupted by a door opening behind them.

A young female CIA operative came in and looked at Kryton.

"Sir, Colonel Lamar wants to speak to you," she said.

Kryton nodded and thanked her, and she left the room. He looked at Dalton.

"Let's see what he wants."

Both men left the relatively narrow confines of the interrogation building and walked outside.

They swiped their access cards and walked out into the open night sky. A cool, gentle ocean breeze swept over their faces. Kryton looked up and stood for a moment, observing the star-filled sky. The moon had already descended for the evening, but there was still a beautiful glow shining down on them.

The noise of several generators humming loudly, along with the movement of a few Humvees, reminded him that he was still at a military outpost.

They both walked approximately one-hundred metres, through a couple of locked gates and to the command centre. They swiped their access cards and entered.

Despite it being a little after midnight in the South Pacific, the staff at the classified site were working to eastern seaboard U.S. time, so the facility was abuzz with movement.

They entered another door and walked into the Secure Compartmented Information Facility. The SCIF. This was the well-protected hub where all the top-secret computers and information displays are kept, along with the sensitive communications equipment.

Although U.S. military operations are planned from the Pentagon, with subordinate commands running designated operations from bases in their part of the world, CIA operations are mobile and run from wherever is most effective, keeping potential adversaries guessing and never knowing what the spies are up to.

This site, hidden somewhere in the middle of the South Pacific, was now the centre of an Allied intelligence operation to determine how the President of the United States almost came to being assassinated.

They moved over to a desk where a man in army camouflage uniform was standing, speaking into an encrypted phone.

Kryton and Dalton waited patiently, observing the myriad of screens and information displays covering the walls.

Kryton looked at the screen showing BBC news. File pictures of Chinese warships steaming in formation were being shown on a loop.

"It's getting serious," said Dalton quietly.

Kryton nodded softly as the man in camouflage put down the phone.

Colonel Joseph Lamar was the senior American military officer at the site. An African-American of very solid build, he was no-nonsense and very intelligent. He worked in liaison with all of the other agencies at the undisclosed location.

"How's it tracking?" he asked Kryton.

"I want to give him another twenty minutes with the noise before I go in," Kryton informed him.

Lamar shook his head.

"You've got to go now. Washington wants a better intelligence picture and they believe he might be the link. They're giving us no more than another four hours before the President makes a decision based on whatever we know by that time."

"Decision?" asked Dalton.

"The President has decided it's time to make a kinetic response, and so far, it looks like the Chinese will be on the receiving end of that," said Lamar.

The two operators glanced at each other.

"But we don't know that it was the Chinese," protested Kryton, "only that some Chinese guys were involved."

Lamar walked over to a large screen that displayed the South China Sea. It had force dispositions of both Chinese and Allied naval vessels on it – just like the one in the Situation Room in Washington.

Lamer pointed to it and explained some of the detail to the two men in front of him.

"I don't know what their exact thinking is in Washington, but the Pentagon has told me that we can expect some specific orders in response soon."

"If this was Chinese sponsored, they would have done more by now," said Kryton, mirroring the advice the Chairman had given the President half a world away.

"Perhaps, but NSA and CIA are picking up all sorts of chatter, most of it conflicting. Our best bet is to find out from someone who was there – and that person is your guy," Lamar said to Kryton, pointing to a small screen in the corner which displayed live CCTV footage from inside the interrogation room.

The Australian nodded in agreement. He'd only known the Colonel for a short time but found him to be competent. Lamar would have liked to have given Kryton more time to really go through the interrogation process and get the Persian to open up, but he was under pressure from his own superiors.

Kryton looked at Dalton.

"Okay, we need to step it up. Do you like poker?"

Dalton looked at him curiously.

"I'm from Texas, of course I like poker."

"Let's go then."

The two men walked towards the door.

Kryton stopped and turned to look back at Lamar.

"Sir, are you in contact with my military headquarters in Australia?" he asked the Colonel.

"Yes. We have channels of communication through liaisons. We're waiting to see what they can get from the Chinese men you detained in Dili," replied Lamar.

"Good. Please keep me informed."

"Looking for anything in particular?" asked Lamar.

Kryton shook his head.

"No. They'll be asking the same sort of questions I am. We'll compare notes, and this will help come up with the best intelligence picture."

"Will do," said the Colonel, giving the thumbs up as he turned to speak to some of the other staff in the SCIF.

Kryton and Dalton left the command centre and walked back across the compound to the interrogation building.

They walked with a sense of urgency. They both knew what was at stake.

"Do you think Lang will pull the trigger and retaliate against the Chinese?" asked Kryton to his American counterpart.

"I just don't know," answered Dalton. "He's always come across as pretty headstrong, but I never took him for being reckless."

"Political pressure is a powerful thing," mused Kryton. "Even my government has jumped in to say they'll unconditionally support the U.S. It could be Iraq all over again."

"Yeah. Which is why we need to work out who actually did this," stated Dalton as they reached the outer door of the interrogation building.

Kryton nodded in agreement.

"Time's short – so let's just get this done."

3

The rusty bolt to the door was unlocked. Two large men intentionally made loud, deliberate and very aggressive noises as they entered, shouting at the top of their lungs indiscriminately.

Their voices, only slightly muffled by the light fabric ski-masks they had covering their faces, now replaced the screaming baby noise which had filled the room for so long.

Two of the men picked Behrouz up by the armpits and placed him forcefully down onto a chair they had brought into the room with them. The first one pulled back on the Persian's hair, forcing his head back to expose his face.

The second man then poured some cold water over his head.

The shock of the water rolling down his face brought Behrouz to life, his eyes now widened and alert.

Another two men came in quickly and noisily; one rolling a trolley which contained a long, flat board with straps, the other carrying two large buckets of icy cold water. They made a deliberate act of placing all the items in front of the detainee.

The large men kept yelling, circling the Persian and shouting into his face. Behrouz looked down and saw the items now laid out in front of him. He gasped in fear.

He struggled in the chair, but a large hand kept him firmly in his seat.

He knew what the items were for.

Kryton and Dalton observed from behind the mirror.

The Australian let the masked men carry on for another minute – his aim being to instil fear into the Persian.

"Okay, it's time," he said to Dalton.

Kryton took a step over to the table in the corner, picked up a large piece of fabric cloth and left the observation room.

He paused for a moment.

He inhaled deeply. A look of steeled resolve now covered his face.

He entered softly and unnoticed.

The men maintained their yelling, forcing the Persian to recoil in shock and fear in his seat.

One of them noticed Kryton. His entry was the signal to take the interrogation to the next step.

What appeared like chaos to Behrouz, who was now starting to fear for his life, was, in fact, a well-planned and choreographed symphony.

And Kryton was one of the best in the business.

One of the men moved around behind Behrouz and pulled his shoulders back. Another pulled on the seated man's hair, forcing his head back so he was now looking up.

Kryton walked over forcefully. He wore no mask. Behrouz already knew what he looked like. He knew this was the man in charge.

"Will you talk?" Kryton asked loudly.

Behrouz's eyes moved from side to side in fear, as if looking for support or help.

"Don't look at them, look at me," Kryton screamed into Behrouz's face.

"Who do you work for?" screamed the Australian.

The Persian gasped, trying to speak.

He didn't get a chance.

"WHO DO YOU WORK FOR?" Kryton screamed again, even louder and more aggressively.

The Persian continued to gasp and squirm. It was futile. His hands and feet were still bound and the large men held him firmly into the chair.

He tried to speak, but the terror made it difficult.

Kryton scrunched the fabric cloth up into a small ball in his fist, dunked it in one of the buckets of water, and held it in front of Behrouz's face.

"Will you talk? WILL YOU TALK?" screamed Kryton.

The Persian let out a large high-pitched scream.

"No, no, please no," he managed to say in between his wailing.

Kryton paused the verbal assault for a moment and kneeled next to Behrouz at a slight angle. One of the large men held Behrouz's head tightly, forcing him to look out of the corner of his eyes at Kryton.

"Well?" said Kryton, in a softer tone this time.

Behrouz continued to gasp, looking alternatively between Kryton and the buckets of water sitting next to the flat board with the straps.

Kryton noticed this. He too looked at the buckets and board, then back at Behrouz.

He gritted his teeth and moved his face closer to Behrouz.

"Last chance. Will-you-talk?" Kryton asked slowly.

Behrouz continued to gasp. His chest heaved as the shock and fear made his body naturally seek more oxygen through heavy breaths.

Kryton looked at the men and nodded.

With rapid efficiency, they removed the binds on the Persian's hands and feet and whisked him down onto the flat board. He struggled with all his might, but after having been bound and seated for several days with little food and water, he was weak and numb.

He cried out in terror.

As quickly as they put him down, the men picked him up again and placed him back onto the chair, retying his hands and feet.

Kryton once again moved in next to his face.

"Will you talk?"

"Yes…yes," said Behrouz, almost crying.

In the observation room behind the mirror, Dalton let out a small chuckle.

"Poker!" he muttered to himself.

"What?" asked the female CIA operative standing next to him, obviously mortified by what she had just witnessed for the first time in her fledgling career.

Dalton looked at her with a sly grin on his face.

"Poker," he said again. "He bluffed – and he won."

The girl stood there with a confused look on her face until the penny dropped.

"You mean. He was never going to waterboard him?"

Dalton looked back through the mirror.

"Nope. He didn't even touch him."

The girl looked horrified. Her face turned a pale white. She excused herself and went outside to throw up.

Dalton watched her leave. He felt a little sorry for her. He returned his gaze to back inside the room, where he saw the large men untying Behrouz's hands and feet.

Kryton quickly exited the interrogation room and joined Dalton.

"Well done!" said the SEAL to his Australian friend.

Kryton looked at him, smiled and softly shrugged his shoulders.

"Well, we know that he's not a professional. He broke like an old rubber band."

"What now?" asked Dalton.

"Have Lamar bring some food and drink over, and some fresh clothing. He'll answer the first few questions out of fear. After that, he'll answer because I'm giving him stuff, so I'll seek to make him comfortable."

"Copy," said Dalton, picking up a phone with his free hand and pressing the button to speak to the command centre.

One of the large men who had assisted Kryton came into the observation room.

"What now, boss?"

"Set up the table and two chairs. One either side. Like in a café," Kryton instructed him.

"And turn the heat down, too."

The large man nodded and went about setting the interrogation room up just like Kryton had directed.

Kryton splashed some water from a bottle over his own face and ran his hand through his hair. Although he had only been in the interrogation room for a relatively short time, it had been long enough to make him start sweating profusely.

He leaned against a table and thought for a moment while Dalton had a conversation with the command centre.

The American hung up the phone.

"They're bringing some stuff over," he said.

"Good."

Kryton stood up to go into the room.

"Push Lamar for the details on this guy. NSA has his picture and some biological and biographical details, and we retrieved his phone and passport in Dili. Surely, they've run it through the databases by now. I'll need something to work with."

Dalton nodded.

"I'm on it."

Kryton took a long, deep breath, then took a sip of water.

Okay, champ, Kryton thought to himself, using an informal Australian soldier term for someone not particularly well regarded, *let's see what you know.*

4

Kryton sat down in a chair opposite Behrouz. The Persian was now facing the back wall. Kryton wanted the detainee to focus only on him.

Kryton's aim now was to build a rapport – to show that he was a friend.

Ostensibly, at least.

He needed to make the detainee comfortable enough to want to share information, but not too comfortable that he would start to lie. Kryton would ensure that throughout the questioning, he would occasionally remind Behrouz that lies would result in more screaming babies.

Kryton had interrogated the worst possible members of the Taliban leaders just as easily as he'd shared bread and chai with them and their families.

It was all just acting.

But it wasn't designed to entertain. It was about eliciting intelligence.

He watched as the timid man before him reached out to a large plate in the middle of the table. It contained a few varieties of breads and fresh fruits. Behrouz slowly picked at some bread and sipped at a plastic cup of water.

Kryton leaned forward and smiled.

"Behrouz, I'm sorry about your leg. Is it okay?" he asked.

The Persian man looked up at Kryton and nodded. There was no anger in his eyes, just the look of a defeated man.

"You see now that we're treating you well, do you agree?" he asked the Persian.

Behrouz again looked up slowly and nodded.

Kryton patted Behrouz's free hand across the table.

"I want to help you, Behrouz. I don't think you're the bad guy in all of this. If you help me to help you, I promise you'll be well looked after."

Kryton picked up a small piece of bread off of the plate.

He knew that the appearance of sharing food with Behrouz would help loosen his tongue – if he was even reluctant to talk at all. He'd seen weaker looking men hold out for days, yet also tougher and harder men break simply by being paraded naked in front of female interrogators.

Everyone had their weak point.

It was almost impossible to determine where it was until people were under the pressure of a skilled interrogator.

Kryton made some small talk about the quality of the food and how good it was that Behrouz was no longer being tied up and exposed to unbearably loud noises.

He allowed Behrouz a few moments to take in some food and water. It would help him think clearly after the sensory deprivation of the past twenty-four hours.

Kryton watched him eat. He felt nothing for the man in front of him, he was just another detainee that might have the information they needed.

Or, he might not.

The Australian leaned forward and took a more serious tone.

"Behrouz, what happens now depends on you. You can help me, or you can choose not to. But you know what will happen if you don't," said Kryton, not too subtly threatening the Persian.

Behrouz paused eating for a moment and glanced at Kryton.

He nodded slightly.

"Okay, then," said Kryton, easing his demeanour somewhat.

"How did you get to Dili? You're obviously not from there."

Behrouz took a sip of water before taking a deep breath.

"I flew in from Dubai, two days before I was supposed to shoot the missile," he said.

"Good, good," said Kryton.

"Where did you fly through?"

Behrouz stayed silent and tried to take a sip of water from the cup.

With the speed of an attacking snake, Kryton reached across the table and knocked it out of his hand. He leaned up over the table aggressively.

"I ask a question; you answer it straight away. Understand?" said Kryton firmly.

Behrouz leaned back in his chair; eyes widened in fear yet again as the imposing Australian stood over him.

"Yes, yes, I'm sorry," he whimpered.

It wasn't that Kryton actually thought the Persian was stalling; it was simply a technique to make Behrouz think that even the slightest perceived delay in answering simple questions would have consequences. It would prevent him from having time to think of lies to say.

Kryton sat down again, looking at Behrouz. He reached over and once again patted him on the hand.

"This is simple, okay," he said softly and reassuringly, again changing tone.

"Where did you fly through?"

"Jakarta. From Dubai, I flew to Jakarta, then into Dili," Behrouz blurted out in what was almost one complete word, fearful not to answer as quickly as possible.

Kryton had intimidated him enough to want to talk.

"How did you get to Dubai?" asked Kryton.

"I flew from Tehran. I live in Iran."

"That's good, Behrouz. Now, you're Persian, and the people you were with were Chinese. Are you a Jihadi?" asked the Australian.

Behrouz started breathing heavily, obviously fearful of giving the wrong answer.

"No. No, I swear to Allah. I am not a jihadi. I am a good Muslim," he pleaded to Kryton.

Kryton looked at him for a moment.

"Then why did you try to shoot down a plane? That's the act of a jihadi. Why are you lying to me?" shouted Kryton.

"No, please, I swear," pleaded Behrouz again, whimpering. "I did it for money. He said he'd pay me for my family."

Kryton thought for a moment. He knew the interrogation was being recorded, and there was a team of analysts in the command centre watching and taking notes; but he had to maintain the mental dexterity to keep abreast of what was being told to him, and then ask the appropriate lines of questions, countering any information that didn't make sense or line up with previous answers, and seeking to determine the difference between the truth and lies.

"Who told you?"

"I don't know, I never met him. I saw an advertisement on the internet. I am like what you call a mercenary," said Behrouz.

"A mercenary? Mercenaries don't shoot down planes full of innocent civilians," countered Kryton.

A confused look appeared on the Persian's face.

"No. No, it was a cargo plane. He said it would have only soldiers on it."

20

Kryton continued chasing details about whoever recruited Behrouz. "What was his name?"

"Peter. He told me to call him Peter," said Behrouz.

"That's a western name. Are you lying to me again?" shouted Kryton.

Behrouz flinched, placing his hands over his face.

He feared Kryton might hit him.

He almost started crying.

Kryton was pushing him because, like a child trying to give excuses to an intimidating parent about something they did, Behrouz was likely to spill as much information as possible in order to ease the pressure coming from the Australian. This would save Kryton from having to ask lots of questions because the information would naturally come out.

"No, I swear. He paid me twenty-thousand American dollars and said that this was the only job. I never met him. The Chinese picked me up at the airport and took me to the house of a Timorese man in Dili."

"What was the name of that man?" asked Kryton firmly.

Behrouz's eyes wandered, like he was genuinely trying to recall the name.

Kryton let him think for a moment. He could tell when someone was stalling, and when someone was actually trying to recall details.

"Alberto. His name was Alberto."

Kryton had a momentary flashback to the previous week in Dili, where he had discovered the Dili Harbour Master shot in his own apartment, and the ensuing chase and fight he had had with one of the Chinese men.

"Yeah, we know that guy. He's dead," Kryton said without the least bit of sympathy. "What about that fat bastard I shot up at the statue. He was Persian, how do you know him?"

"I didn't," said Behrouz, "I only met him for the first time in Dili. I didn't even know his full name. I called him Fatim."

"What about the man who recruited you, this guy called Peter. How did he pay you?" the Australian continued.

"He said he'd transfer the money to my bank account. Half before I flew to Dili, and then half after. Please, I only wanted to help my family," said Behrouz, clearly starting to realise the gravity of the situation he was in.

Kryton stood up and paced around the table. This was to allow himself a moment to consider the information he had obtained so far.

The Persian continued to sit slumped in his chair, tears streaming down his face.

The recruiter, Peter. Kryton wanted to know more about him.

He sat down again in his chair.

"Look at me," he said to Behrouz. "Tell me more about Peter. How many times have you spoken to him?"

Behrouz thought for a moment.

"We exchanged a few emails. I only spoke to him once."

"When?"

The day I landed in Dili. The Chinese man who picked me up had handed me his phone and then Peter asked if I was ready. I told him yes. At this point, he said he'd transfer some money to my account."

Kryton was about to speak when a small flashing light appeared above the door.

"Okay, Behrouz. This is good. I'm going outside for a moment. I'll get you some more water, okay!"

Behrouz let out a small, timid smile. He still had fear in his eyes, but Kryton had been successful in getting him to begin to talk.

Kryton looked at Behrouz for a moment. He noticed his outstretched fingers pulled up by his chest.

The tips were a tinge of yellow.

"Would you like a cigarette?" Kryton asked him.

Behrouz looked straight at Kryton, hopefully.

"Yes, I would very much like one. Please."

Kryton nodded, stood up from his chair and pated Behrouz on the shoulder as he walked past him towards the door.

The rusty hinges made a squealing noise as he walked through.

He entered the observation room, where Dalton and several CIA observers had been watching.

"What's up? I'm only just starting," queried Kryton.

Dalton looked at him with a bemused look on his face.

"You've been in there for ninety minutes," said Dalton.

"Oh," exclaimed Kryton.

Dalton looked at Kryton with some sympathy – his new Australian friend hadn't slept for nearly two and a half days.

Kryton splashed some water on his face.

"What have you got?" he asked Dalton, knowing that the American wouldn't have pulled him out halfway through an interrogation unless it was important.

"The NSA has completed stripping his phone, and we've pulled quite a bit of information," Dalton informed him, using the informal term to describe how the technicians had been able to retrieve lots of data from Behrouz's phone.

"Excellent. What else?" asked Kryton.

"Our CIA friends here have also been able to work out more about this guy's background," Dalton said, handing Kryton a small dossier that they had been crudely assembled.

Kryton flipped through the pages.

This made him smile. It would help disprove or corroborate the answers Behrouz was giving him.

One of the CIA operatives started detailing what they knew for Kryton.

"He's telling the truth about his recent travel history," said the CIA operator. "We were able to trace the passport he had and his recent movements. He's been on a watch list in the United Arab Emirates for some time, mostly due to his activities supporting militia groups fighting in Iraq and some other mercenary activity. He's also a former Iranian Army soldier."

Kryton nodded while looking at the pages in his hand.

"This guy's pretty low level, all said and done. But –" continued the operator.

"But, what?" asked Kryton.

"But the passport is false, and his travel route was done in a way that suggests someone knew how to get him through different airports without alerting the watch lists."

Kryton looked at Dalton, raising his eyebrows curiously.

"So how was he able to travel out of Dubai?" asked Kryton.

"He's actual name is Behrouz Iravani. He used the name *Bachar* on the Iranian passport he used to travel to Jakarta. UAE intelligence didn't have his biographical details listed, so they were only looking for a name, not any physical descriptions. They didn't know about any aliases," continued the operative.

"How did you work out his actual name, then?" asked Kryton.

"Jordanian intelligence had more detail on him. We've been asking all our allies in the region."

"The information we've received from our allies in the Middle East suggests he isn't a high-end professional. At best just a guy with some military training and a desire to make some money," added Dalton.

Kryton ran his hands through his hair, trying to make sense of all the information.

"That lines up with what I'm seeing in there," he said.

The Australian stood looking through the window at Behrouz, who was sitting still in his chair facing the opposite wall.

"So, he's not a professional. But he's getting professional support. The passport, the travel. I'm guessing he's only a small fish in this," mused Kryton.

He turned to look at the same CIA operative who had provided the dossier.

"What's your plans with him after all this?"

The CIA operative looked at Kryton almost in disbelief, until he remembered he was talking to an Australian – a man from a country whose procedures for managing terrorists were a bit different to the U.S. ones.

"He tried to shoot down Air Force One. He's not going home for a long time," said the American drolly.

Kryton looked at him and nodded, realising himself that he'd already known the answer.

Suddenly, a look of inspiration appeared on Kryton's face.

"What is it?" asked Dalton.

"Shit. I haven't yet asked him –" said Kryton before breaking off mid-sentence and running back into the interrogation room.

He walked across the room quickly and sat down in front of the Persian.

Behrouz looked up at him.

"Behrouz, what nationality is Peter?"

"I'm not sure. I told you, I've never met him," said Behrouz.

"You said you spoke to him. What accent did he have?"

Behrouz just looked at Kryton, as if he assumed that they already knew that information.

"He is an American."

Kryton sat back in his seat and had to catch himself from overtly looking like he'd not expected that answer.

Even though he hadn't.

Holding emotions close to your chest is a key tenet of an interrogator.

"Behrouz. You said Peter was going to pay you the rest of the money after the attack. How were you going to get out of Dili?"

Behrouz took a deep breath and sat forward in his chair.

24

"The Chinese men said they would take care of that, but I didn't know how. They didn't tell me."

"So, you went in without knowing how you were going to get out?" asked Kryton in a bemused manner.

Behrouz looked at him, almost sheepishly. His naivety was obvious.

"I just wanted money," he said quietly.

Kryton looked at the pitiful figure in front of him.

He didn't feel sorry for him though.

He might have been a small fish in whatever this situation was, but the dossier detailed a man who'd been involved in murders and the killing of innocent people.

Kryton pulled a pack of cigarettes out of his pocket. He offered one to Behrouz, who graciously took it out of the packet before placing it in his mouth. Kryton lit it for him.

Behrouz inhaled long and deeply, like a seasoned smoker.

Kryton knew time was short, and they needed to send a report to Washington.

He looked at Behrouz, who had already almost finished the first cigarette.

Kryton pulled another from the packet and gave it to the Persian.

Once again, Kryton lit it for him. The Australian sat in the chair for a moment in silence, just staring at Behrouz.

"Behrouz. What would you say if I told you the plane you almost shot down was carrying the President of the United States?"

The Persian froze, nearly choking on the cigarette, before looking back up at Kryton. The realisation of the severity of what this meant was written all over his face – he now knew he wouldn't be going home for a long time.

It confirmed for Kryton that Behrouz wasn't a big player.

Kryton placed the pack of cigarettes on the table, winked at Behrouz, got up and walked out of the room.

5

Kryton walked into the compound dining facility – or DFAC, for short – with Dalton. It was a small facility being run by the U.S. Army caterers, as opposed to the civilian contractors that usually managed most U.S. DFACs globally.

It made sense that army caterers were in charge. After all, this DFAC was at a place that technically didn't exist.

The two men grabbed a plate, walked along the buffet line and took some food from the several choices available.

Kryton had always admired how well the U.S. Army looked after its deployed personnel. An army marches on its stomach, as the saying goes.

Although only a small facility, it operated twenty-four hours a day, seven days a week.

Kryton took a chocolate milk from the drink refrigerator. He felt he had earned it.

The two men went to the back corner of the facility to find a quiet space to talk.

"Lamar wants us in the command centre in ten minutes," said Dalton.

Kryton nodded while playing with some sort of fish with his fork. He'd never trusted DFAC fish while in the Middle East, but he figured that since they were in the middle of the ocean and it was likely to actually be fresh, he could probably eat it.

He smothered it in Tabasco sauce, though, just to be safe.

"What do you think about it all?" asked Dalton.

"I'm confident he's a no-one. He broke very quickly and it's obvious he had no information of real value apart from the name of his contact. Poor guy just answered the wrong ad," Kryton said.

"Who is the American, though?" posed Dalton.

Kryton drank from his chocolate milk. It was an American brand he had never tasted before, but he instantly liked it.

"No idea. But it's interesting. Hopefully whatever the NSA has stripped from the guy's phone can get a lead for us."

Dalton looked around the room. The television was still playing footage about both U.S. and Chinese military movements in the Pacific region.

"It doesn't make sense. What looked like a Chinese action, with their guys in Dili and the submarine that disappeared a few days before, now seems very multi-national," said Dalton.

Kryton nodded in agreement.

"Why hire an Iranian, though? For deniability?" he suggested.

"They weren't expecting him to be caught," suggested Dalton.

They both looked at the television.

"Perhaps it's a North Korean conspiracy?" suggested Kryton satirically.

Dalton conceded a small laugh. He knew that whenever U.S. national agencies couldn't quite work out something that was occurring in the geopolitical environment, they always seemed to point the finger at the North Koreans just to have someone to blame.

The world always needed a bad guy. It came in handy when the agencies were seeking funds at budget time.

"Seriously though," said Kryton, "we'll have to see what my guys can get from those Chinese blokes they're questioning in Dili."

"It's a shame we couldn't bring them here," lamented Dalton.

Kryton tilted his head slightly as he ate a bit more of his food. He spoke as he finished the final few morsels of the rather bland serving.

"Last I heard, although the Chinese are officially denying any involvement, they've still been asking about those guys. That means they *are* Chinese nationals. How would it look if we bring them to a place like this?" he said.

Dalton smiled in understanding as he moved some of the food around on his own plate.

"So, what do you think?"

Kryton thought for a moment.

"If it *was* state-sponsored, I wouldn't put it past the Chinese to disown those guys in Dili. I hear they have some pretty ruthless covert operations arms in the MSS," he said, referring to the Ministry of State Security – the Chinese foreign intelligence agency.

"Very 'Treadstone' like," observed Dalton, referring to the fictional spy program in the *Jason Bourne* movies.

"But all too real," said Kryton. "Which makes me think, if they aren't behind it, then that's why they're trying to talk to those guys – to find out who they are, and what they're doing. The region is on the verge of war, and the media narrative currently has it looking like the Chinese are responsible for it."

Dalton looked up at Kryton, before looking again at the television. It showed footage of Chinese naval fighter aircraft taking off from their sole operational aircraft carrier.

"I think they're scared. And if my eastern martial philosophy doesn't fail me, they'll adhere to the mantra of the best form of defence is attack," said the Australian.

He sighed deeply and stifled a yawn. The thought of regional conflict between two nuclear-armed powers was truly frightening.

"Which means, we need to find out who's actually behind this," Kryton said as the two stood up to leave the DFAC.

They looked at the television again. It didn't paint a pretty picture.

"And fast."

6

Kryton and Dalton walked into the command centre just as the first sign of morning nautical twilight was creeping over the horizon. It had been almost two days since they had both had any form of sleep.

The same could be said for most of the staff in the SCIF.

Colonel Lamar saw the two men enter.

He waved over at Kryton, signalling for the Australian to join him.

"Sir?" said Kryton.

The Colonel handed a file to one of the SCIF staff before giving his full attention to the operator.

"You've got a message," the officer said, handing a small note to Kryton.

Kryton looked over it quickly. His eyes widened in joy.

"Have you been briefed on all these details from my chat with the detainee?" Kryton asked Lamar.

"Yes," replied the Colonel. "We've got all the liaisons fusing the information at the moment," he said, pointing to a large work table in the corner of the SCIF.

The analysts, representing all the key intelligence and military agencies providing support to the unfolding situation, looked tired. Despite this, they were hurriedly working away – tapping on computers and talking on secured phones back to their respective headquarters.

"What is it?" asked Dalton, looking over Kryton's shoulder.

"Some more answers," replied Kryton, waving the note up by his head.

Kryton walked a few paces to a desk that had a secured phone on top of it. He picked up the receiver, placed it next to his ear and pressed a few buttons.

"The Timorese government gave us access to the Chinese guys we had the run-in with in Dili, on the proviso they could observe the 'questioning'," Kryton said to Dalton using inverted air quotes with his free hand.

"Questioning?" queried Dalton, unconvinced by Kryton's statement.

The Australian smiled.

"If we're on a declared operation, it's 'interrogation'. Up until then, it's 'questioning'," said Kryton, winking at the SEAL.

"That's about how we get around the legal side of it, too," mused Dalton as he took a seat in a chair next to Kryton.

The dial tone made a few sharp pitched noises, indicating that it was connecting through to another phone via encrypted satellites.

Several thousand kilometres away, in a large isolated and secure building on the outskirts of the Australian capital of Canberra, sat the Joint Operations Command of the Australian Defence Force – JOC.

This command, literally built in a sheep paddock, was where all ADF operations globally were planned and run from.

"JOC – watchkeeper," came the brief answer from the young, female voice on the other end of the line.

"This is Sergeant Kryton, I need to be transferred to the exploitation team in Dili. Code number is seven – five – three," said Kryton.

"Roger, Sarge. One moment please," came the polite reply.

The sound of more sharp beeps came through the receiver.

More satellites took up the call.

"This is Sergeant Clemente," came another voice down the phone, speaking from a secured site in Dili.

Kryton tilted his head with a curious look on his face.

"Clemo?" he asked.

"Yeah, who's this?"

A big smile appeared on Kryton's face.

"Mate, it's Kryton. I'm at site one," he said familiarly.

"Oh wow, how are you, mate? I heard an Aussie was leading the interrogation there," replied Sergeant Dan Clemente of the Australian Intelligence Corps, Kryton's former branch of the army.

"Great mate, long time," replied Kryton.

The two had worked together on more than one occasion and were trusted colleagues.

"Clemo, I'd love to catch up, but as you can imagine we've got a bit going on here. I know you've sent the report through, can you give me the salient points?"

"No worries. The guy you called 'the Boss' is a professional. He said nothing, not much more than a name and some bullshit about being a fisherman. He had no identification on him and we're at the limit of what we can under this cover. Maybe with more time, we could force him to talk," Clemo informed Kryton.

"What cover are you using?" asked Kryton.

"Federal Police," replied Clemo, referring to the Australian Federal Police – AFP. The Australian equivalent to the FBI.

The Australian Army has some of the best interrogators in the world, yet the term and practice doesn't always sit well with the public, and so they're not supposed to use their skills in times other than war. An interrogation team conducting non-declared operations overseas would have to disguise their activities using a cover. Unfortunately, that limits what actions they can perform, as it would have to be in line with the cover they're using.

The AFP wouldn't be threatening a detainee with waterboarding.

Their Timorese hosts wouldn't even be aware of their true identity.

"And the other one?" asked Kryton, asking about the second Chinese man detained at the doctor's office.

A small laugh came through the receiver.

"Well, it was hard to understand him," said Clemo, "that knock you gave him loosened a few of his teeth. But, once he started talking, we were able to get some good information of value."

Kryton placed the receiver back onto the base of the phone and pressed a button, placing the phone into speaker mode.

"Mate, you're on speaker. My American colleague, Clay Dalton, is here, too."

"G'day, Clay," said Clemo in an intentionally rhythmical way.

Dalton smiled and shook his head, rolling his eyes. Kryton shrugged his shoulders, suggesting to the American that he just accept Clemo's humour.

"Right, he first said that he's just a smuggler. He said that he thought he was smuggling drugs and black-market supplies into Dili," said Clemo.

Kryton and Dalton looked at each other.

"Bullshit. They couldn't even get their stories lined-up," muttered Dalton.

"That's what we thought, so we told him that the attack was on Air Force One, and that that made him a terrorist in the eyes of the international community. Once I got him thinking that his next stop was probably Guantanamo Bay, he started talking."

"Good work. So, what did he give us?" asked Kryton.

"He said his name is Yuan and that he's Chinese Navy, but was recruited to do a special mission of smuggling weapons into Timor-Leste. He's got no identification on him either. He said he gave his passport over to the Boss. He actually seemed genuinely unaware of the Stinger missiles and the plan to attack the President."

"We know the Chinese have been lightly smuggling weapons into the region to get around some arms controls treaties," said Dalton to Kryton.

"And his movements into Dili?" asked Kryton.

The sound of ruffling paper could be heard through the intermittent static on the phone. Clemo was obviously looking through some notes.

"Umm, he says that he flew into Dili from Jakarta, having flown directly from Beijing. He said he was recruited by a senior PLA officer, but that it was all very secretive," said Clemo.

"What about their exit plans from Timor?" asked Kryton.

"He said he didn't know. The Boss was supposed to have that planned out. I think he was being kept on a need to know basis. He and his colleague, the one your commando mate waxed, had just been told to meet the Boss at the wharf in Dili," briefed Clemo.

Kryton sat down next to Dalton and sighed heavily.

Thoughts raced through his head.

He looked at Dalton for his opinion.

"It ties in with what the Persian said. Sounds like they're just lackies in this," suggested the SEAL.

"You think he's MSS?" Kryton asked Clemo down the phone.

"Ha. I doubt it mate, based only on his lack of resilience to our questions. The Boss might be, so we're going to keep working on him."

Kryton looked at Dalton, who he could tell also had thoughts racing through his head.

"It's definitely some sort of intelligence style operation," said Clemo.

"I agree," said Kryton. "Sounds like they've hired some people in order to keep it deniable, just in case they were caught."

"Are you thinking a false flag operation?" asked Clemo, referring to any intelligence operation where one country makes it look like another has carried out the activity.

"Maybe. But we need to look at the bigger picture still," said Kryton. "Clemo, who is conducting the exploitation of everything pulled from those guys?"

"It's all been transferred to the Americans," Clemo replied.

Kryton looked over at the table of analysts working furiously over maps, computers and other bits of information – all eagerly trying to build an intelligence picture to brief back to Washington.

Kryton looked at Dalton, seeking any further questions for Clemo.

The SEAL just shook his head as he leaned forward, the palm of his non-injured side covering his mouth. He looked exhausted.

"Okay, thanks Clemo. Keep us informed of any developments. I'll buy you a beer next time we're back in the old unit in Brisbane," said Kryton as he thanked his friend.

"Will do," replied Clemo, before the audible click indicated the call had ended.

"Nice guy," said Dalton, as the two men walked over to where the analysts were all working.

"Yeah, one of our best interrogators. We served in Afghanistan together. He could get a mannequin to talk – given the right circumstances and enough time!" joked Kryton.

The two operators stood next to Colonel Lamar.

"Washington wants a brief ready in sixty minutes. I'll let these guys play around for another half-hour, then we'll have to send it off," said the U.S. officer, who understood that several checks would have to be made to any brief before it would be put before the President.

Kryton nodded while stifling a yawn.

Lamar smiled softly in empathy.

"There's not much to do now – try to get some rest," offered the Colonel.

The Australian looked at Dalton, who appeared very keen to take the Colonel's offer.

"I saw a couch in that other room that had our names on it," said Kryton.

"Dibs on big spoon," joked Dalton.

Kryton just looked at him in humorous disdain as they walked out of the SCIF.

The two men threw themselves down onto the old leather couch in a small room that was obviously the improvised recreational area. They placed their feet up on a homemade coffee table. The television was showing even more footage, this time it was displaying the morning news from Australia.

After a minute, Dalton picked up the remote control from the coffee table and placed the television on mute.

"I'm happy to have an hour or two without that," he said.
Kryton didn't even hear him.
He'd already nodded off.

7

A young female analyst swiped her access card before opening the heavy door. She proceeded to walk through a small room, before swiping her card yet again and proceeding through another door.

She was tall and slender, wearing neat business attire suitable for a mid-level position at the agency.

Wearing a knee-length red skirt, she had loosened her blouse buttons enough to enjoy the relatively relaxed environment of the sub-basement level she was now on.

She closed the door behind her, and stood at the entrance of the large, air-sealed room.

Several rows of table-top computers were surrounded by three walls of large supercomputers. Small, bright flashing lights flickered through the black veneer of the protective coverings, indicating their operation. The low buzz of cooling fans ensured these supercomputers didn't overheat.

She walked over to where a colleague was sitting. Both were members of the NSA's deep-cyber encryption centre.

The large computers were capable of processing literally millions of algorithms per second. Their sole job was to decipher codes.

Right now, almost all of them were being used to identify the details surrounding how a cyber-attack on Air Force One had been able to occur.

She sat down in an ergonomic swivel chair.

"Hi Alex, try the seven of spades!" she said to the young man who was playing solitaire on his laptop computer. His desk looked like something that belonged in a teenage video gamer's bedroom rather than a highly professional data encryption centre. Packets of chips, gaming magazines and cans of soft drink littered it. Wearing tattered jeans and a

Nintendo t-shirt, he was absolutely making the most of the relaxed environment of his office space.

"Oh, hey Steph," he replied, having been caught unaware by his supervisor.

Although he looked like he should still have been in high school, Alex was in-fact one of the brightest young graduate recruits that the NSA had taken on in recent years.

His supervisor, Steph, also a graduate of the prestigious Massachusetts Institute of Technology, was not that much older than him.

"How's it going?" she asked looking at the second monitor on his table, which displayed the readouts that the supercomputers were generating.

He minimised the game on the laptop and sat up in his chair. He respected her and wanted to give her his full attention.

"It's processing everything the air force electronics computer technicians provided to us. It's a complicated algorithm, like one I've never seen before," he briefed her.

She looked closely at the numbers and data displayed on the computer monitor. It would only have made sense to a very few, very bright people.

It's the reason why they had been recruited.

"How long?" she asked.

"Well theoretically, based on all the known number of algorithms that could be used, exponentially, for computer codes, this thing could process forever and we might never actually decrypt it enough to work out the origins of the attack."

"But we know that the attack originated from somewhere in the South China Sea," she said.

"Yes. We're comparing it to all known codes that have been used in previous hacking attacks. This data extraction will tell us how the attack was able to penetrate some of the most secure software in the world which they had embedded onboard."

"Some sort of advanced coding or encryption beating software?" she suggested.

He shook his head as he took a sip from the nearly empty can of Pepsi.

"Unlikely, we're all over the latest advancements. We're the ones writing the most advanced codes, and even we have trouble hacking wirelessly into our defensive software. These algorithms look as advanced as any of that that our people have been writing."

She sat back into the chair.

"Well, we've always got people trying to steal our secrets. They can't always rely on another Edward Snowden giving them to them. Perhaps they've learned some advanced hacking processes," she stated, referring to the infamous former NSA employee who managed to smuggle highly classified secrets out of agency computers before fleeing to Russia.

He smiled as the computers continued processing the data that had been taken from off of the systems onboard Air Force One.

"It would be a hell of a way to announce it if someone had come up with something new," he said.

She laughed in acknowledgement.

The rest of the room was empty. Although usually filled with analysts processing and deciphering encrypted algorithms, most were at lunch or on assignment on other duties.

"How long have you been down here for?" she asked him.

He ran his hands through his shaggy mop of hair, before subconsciously rubbing his eyes.

"About fourteen hours now," he replied.

"Oh, Alex, we're not that short of people. You need to get some rest."

"I'm okay. Besides, do you know who else can understand all this stuff?" he said pointing to the supercomputer wall.

She tilted her head to the side and just shrugged her shoulders, before shaking her head.

"No," she conceded.

It wasn't that Alex was cocky; it was just that he was the best in the NSA at understanding and deciphering foreign codes.

"It would be nice to have windows in this place," she observed, looking around as she stood up to leave. She stretched her arms out and yawned, obviously as tired as any of them from the past few days.

"Can I get you anything?" she asked him.

Alex sat frozen in his chair, looking straight at his screen.

"Hello. Earth to Alex," she said, waving her hand in front of his face to bring him back to the present.

His eyes shot up at her.

"Window!" he said softly, thoughts obviously racing through his head.

She looked at him, confused.

He launched himself upright in his chair and started tapping at the keyboard on his computer. He simultaneously picked up the handset of a secured phone. He pressed a single button.

He spoke the moment someone picked up on the other end.

"Mars? It's Jupiter. I'm coming down now and we need a priority assessment on a code we've got. I'm bringing Athena with me."

Steph rolled her eyes. She hated the names these computer geeks gave each other. She wasn't particularly fond of the name they had used for her.

Athena – the Greek goddess of wisdom and warfare. It was actually the name the analyst team used for the person in her position, a bit like the character 'M' in the *James Bond* movies.

Alex hung up the phone. He placed a USB stick into the side of his computer, downloaded some information onto it, then ripped it out and jumped up.

Steph was grateful she had changed her high heels for the comfort of flats, as she struggled to keep up with Alex as he made a beeline through the secure doors and out of the room.

Twenty minutes later, the two of them were waiting outside of the offensive cyber operations centre within the NSA. A separate department, it was responsible for conducting offensive cyber operations globally. Their most recent success had been conducting psychological warfare using social media against ISIS in the Middle-East, but their remit also extended to trying to disrupt North Korean cyber activity, as well as maintaining an eye on Chinese and Russian state-sponsored cyber advancements.

"What is it?" pressed Steph for what felt like the hundredth time. She still didn't know what was going on.

After the Snowden incident, NSA employees had been further restricted from areas not directly within their remit, and so the two of them wouldn't be able to have direct access to that area. The departments still worked closely, though.

Alex was pacing back and forth, his computer-like brain was running in circles.

She sat on a chair and decided to just let him pace.

A few minutes later, a door opened and a man stepped out. It was Mars. Not much older than Alex, he at least made the effort to wear a collar and tie, even if it was mismatched with stonewash denim jeans and Converse sneakers.

38

He looked nervous.

Steph stood up, and the three formed a close circle. Even though they were in one of the most secure buildings in the world, Mars spoke softly, as if the very noise of their conversation was breaching state secrets or being listened to. The analysts at most signals-intelligence agencies were like that – deeply paranoid, even to the extent of distrusting their own.

"Your theory was right," started Mars, "we ran it through our research and development systems, and the code was in there."

Alex's face started turning white.

"In there? What does that mean?" asked Steph, still trying to catch up.

Alex looked at her, remembering that she was the supervisor and that she would need to be the one to take this higher.

"It means the code embedded onto the plane that enabled the compromise is ours."

Steph's eyes widened.

"What? But how?"

Mars, being the expert in offensive cyber coding, answered.

"It had a window in it. The code was embedded with what we call a 'communications window'. It means that it was able to sit in the computer systems on Air Force One without being suspected, because all the algorithms in the code were friendly ones that matched our protocols. Nothing about it would have looked suspicious to the network's virus protection systems."

"So, what did the window do?" asked Steph.

"Well," replied Alex, "we think that it was connected into the navigation systems and that the program was written to shut down the plane's network firewalls at a designated location. Air Force One is basically just one big computer network."

Steph nodded that she understood.

"The code itself wasn't malicious – the network would have picked up on it otherwise. It was designed to trick the network into thinking that it was about to undergo some sort of checks or routine maintenance. Once the firewalls were down, someone was able to hack in remotely and wreak havoc," continued Mars.

"We know that the hack came from the South China Sea somewhere," she said. "What does that tell us?"

"Well, the signals transmissions team have managed to locate the origin, so we know where the hack was transmitted from. However –"

Steph looked at the two analysts, who appeared to be having a telepathic conversation.

"However?" she asked, by now almost frustrated with them and how quickly they were able to think.

"However, it means that someone had to have written the code *and* loaded it into Air Force One's network," added Alex. "And that could only have been done from inside this building."

Steph gasped as she covered her mouth with her left palm.

"The plane was sabotaged?" she asked.

"Looks like it," said Mars. "But, why would they leave such an obvious trace? I mean, you were never going to find the code in the decryption computers because they're not foreign algorithms, but we were able to trace it relatively easy through our offensive algorithm systems."

"That's because we were never supposed to find the code. The plane was supposed to be a smoking wreck in the ocean," said Alex. "No trace would have been left to conduct this type of forensic investigation."

"Shit," whispered Steph.

Mars handed Alex back the USB.

"I've got to go," he said, "my boss is already shutting everything else down to start looking at this, and what other compromises we might have. This is big."

"Thanks, Mars," said Steph, before the young analyst swiped his access card and walked back into his workspace.

"What now?" asked Alex, looking genuinely nervous.

Steph stood for a moment, thinking.

"Someone in the NSA is a traitor," she said.

She sighed heavily. She knew this could have serious ramifications – a potential insider working against U.S. interests.

"Do you have a comb and a jacket?" she asked Alex.

He nodded, unsure why she was asking.

"Good. Go get them. We're going to have to brief the General."

8

President Jack Lang stood outside of the Situation Room in discussion with Secretary of State Bradley Kingston. The two men were on the verge of exhaustion. Neither had had much sleep since nearly being shot down over Timor-Leste just under a week earlier.

He looked over some pictures that the Defence Department had provided him earlier. Secretary Kingston looked over his shoulder.

They showed outlines of what appeared to be small coral islands.

Several of them had ships at anchor nearby.

"This is current?" the President asked.

"Yes, sir. Admiral Pike will brief you on them inside the room," replied the Secretary.

Waiting inside for the President were his staff, as well as most of the heads of the seventeen agencies that comprised the U.S. intelligence community.

He took in a deep breath, adjusted his tie and stepped forward.

A neatly dressed Marine opened the door for him.

He walked in purposefully, followed by the Secretary.

"Ten-HUT," came the command from Admiral Pike, standing at the other end of the room.

The verbal command was ostensibly to call to attention the military personnel in the room to respond to the presence of their Commander-in-Chief, but protocol meant that everyone stood up when the boss walked in.

President Lang took a seat. He didn't want to waste time.

"Admiral – go," he said simply.

"Mister President, the following intelligence brief summaries what we know with inputs from all U.S. agencies, as well as contributions from various nations in the Pacific."

41

The Chairman of the Joint Chiefs placed his wooden pointer to one of the maps on the television screen.

"Sir, the Chinese fleet movements that I briefed this morning haven't significantly changed throughout the day. Our assessment now is that they're taking defensive positions in anticipation of our actions."

The President looked at the screen closely, which showed known Chinese and Allied military positions across the South China Sea and the Western Pacific.

The Admiral continued briefing.

"The NSA has managed to identify the location of the island where the communication directing the cyber-attack on Air Force One occurred from," he said.

The President sat up a little higher in his leather chair. This was of great interest to him.

The screen instantly zoomed in, showing a small, narrow island in the southern part of the South China Sea. The north-eastern part had a small harbour inlet with a wharf, whilst the southern part of the island had several steep, tree-covered rocky hills. A coral reef protected the southern end, whilst the western side had a long stretch of sand that appeared to have some decent looking waves, probably suitable for surfing.

"Keyhole satellite imagery taken several hours ago indicates the presence of what appears to be a small military outpost on the eastern side of this unnamed island, next to a small harbour with a wharf," briefed the Admiral as he pointed to the image on the screen.

"We've tentatively named this island 'Zulu One'," continued the Admiral.

The audience looked in closely.

"It doesn't have a name already?" asked the President.

"Sir, it's so small and remote that it's barely on most of our maps."

"Is this Chinese controlled?" asked the Secretary.

"It's not one of the islands we know to have been taken over by the Chinese as part of their forced acquisition of islands in the region," said the Admiral.

"What makes us think it's a military outpost?" asked the President.

Director Blake stepped in to answer.

"We've been able to triangulate and link various communications from that island to several phones confiscated from the suspects detained in Dili, as well as to some communications from a Chinese submarine that fell out of our sonar nets in recent weeks."

The President looked at the Secretary in a bemused but equally impressed way, then back at the NSA Director. He was an intelligent man, but he knew better than to ask about the technical side of how the NSA conducted its activities.

"The same submarine that we believe smuggled the Stinger missiles into Timor-Leste?" asked the President.

"Yes, sir."

"Have we reacquired or located that submarine?" asked President Lang.

The Admiral pointed to the screen as it zoomed in onto the small harbour.

The image now on the screen, although somewhat grainy, was clear enough to show the outline of several small huts with multiple communications towers and arrays nearby. At the end of the small wharf which jutted out into the harbour was the distinct image of a sleek, black tube-like object.

"This, sir," said the Admiral pointing to the object, "is a Chinese *Ming* class diesel-electric submarine."

The President sat back in his chair and loosened his tie.

"Do we know names? Details?" asked the Secretary.

"No, sir," replied the Admiral. "The weather conditions haven't been conducive to a clearer image."

"So, we're sure this island is involved in directing the cyber-attack?" the President asked Director Blake.

"Yes, sir. One-hundred percent."

"But we're not sure if it's a declared Chinese military outpost?"

"No, sir."

"Why not? There's a Chinese submarine there, right?" asked the President, confused.

CIA Director Anna Dawn turned in her chair to speak.

"As the Admiral said, sir, our intelligence suggests that this island isn't part of the recent acquisition in the area by the Chinese," she said.

She looked down at some notes before looking back at the President and continuing.

"Additionally, through our various back-channels and through analysis by naval intelligence, we've been able to ascertain that the Chinese Navy has, sometime in the past twelve months, had a submarine mysteriously removed from their ORBAT," she said, referring to the Chinese order of battle – essentially an inventory of their active military equipment.

"As in decommissioned?" asked the Secretary.

"No," said the Admiral, "removed – meaning that for all intents and purposes, it's lost. They don't know where it is."

"Jesus Christ," muttered the President.

The staff at the table started to chatter amongst themselves before President Lang placed his hands up to quieten the audience.

"Let me guess – A *Ming* class submarine."

"Yes, sir," said the Admiral.

The President leaned forward in his chair and placed both of his palms over his face. He felt like he was ageing several years every day.

"What's our assessment of all this, then?" he asked the room generally.

No-one said anything immediately, until the NSA Director spoke up.

"The Chinese are still flatly denying involvement – but we'd expect them to. What has me puzzled is that nothing in the intelligence we *do* have supports the theory of some in this room that they *were* involved. We just don't have anything to firmly prove who was responsible for this."

"We *do* have the evidence," interjected the Secretary. "I think these fleet movements are very provocative, and the communications have Chinese fingerprints all over them."

The President quietly placed his hand on the Secretary's arm. He could tell his friend and trusted advisor was getting emotional. He didn't blame him, though, not after what had almost happened.

"What about other sources, then? Terrorists, other state actors? How about North Korea even?" asked the President.

"I don't believe so, sir, not with the complexities of the resources we know have been involved," said the CIA Director.

The President started quietly whispering to the Secretary, words inaudible to the rest of those present in the room.

The senior officials at the table started talking to themselves or writing notes onto the notepads in their leather-bound folders.

The President could tell that there still wasn't a consensus amongst his officials.

"Who of our allies has this same information?" he asked.

"The Australians have provided much of the signals-intelligence, shared under the five-eyes agreement," said Director Blake, referring to the intelligence-sharing arrangements between the U.S. U.K, Australia, Canada, and New Zealand.

"What's their opinion?"

"They've offered to support us militarily and with intelligence as it becomes available, sir," replied the NSA Director.

"So, we need to know more about *that* island and what's on it, to improve our intelligence picture," said the President firmly.

The key staff sitting around the table nodded in agreement.

The President sat back in his chair and ran his hand through his thinning hair.

"How do we go about this?" he asked.

"Mister President – Director Dawn, Admiral Pike and I have an idea. We'd like to brief you in the tight-five," said Director Blake.

"Understood," replied the President. "Right, we keep our fleet where it is on standby for now. Just because the Chinese are doing nothing now doesn't mean that they won't. Remember, these are people with a culture that is founded on the principles of patience and playing the long game."

He looked at the Secretary, who was stifling a small yawn.

"Tight-five in the Oval Office in ten minutes," he said.

The Secretary nodded.

President Lang stood up. The room immediately did the same.

"We'll focus on this island as a priority, but I don't want us to take our eyes off other possibilities. There are no stupid ideas in this."

He looked around the faces in the room. They all looked like he felt.

"Ensure your people are getting rest. I don't want anything missed because we failed to manage ourselves," he said sympathetically.

President Lang and Secretary Kingston walked out of the room. They walked quickly to the Oval Office – even the two U.S. Secret Service agents assigned to the President's detail struggled to keep up.

"So, what are Blake and Dawn cooking up?" asked President Lang as they powered up the long, narrow hallways of the sub-basement of the White House. Pictures of U.S. military equipment and portraits of famous American political leaders, mostly from the Revolutionary and Civil Wars, adorned the walls.

"Not sure," responded the Secretary, "but if they wanted it in the tight-five, you know it's high level."

The 'tight-five' was the informal term the President used to describe the small group he discussed the most classified national security issues with. It included Admiral Pike, both the NSA and CIA Directors, as well as Secretary Kingston. President Lang had personally appointed both Blake and Dawn, and they had been easily confirmed by the U.S. Senate.

He trusted all of them implicitly.

He would have to now.

9

"Will there be anything else, sir?" asked the White House steward as he placed several glasses of scotch and ice down on the coffee table in the middle of the Oval Office.

"No, Mister Johnson, thank you though," replied the President politely to his longest-serving and most trusted steward. Sidney Johnson had served presidents as far back as Jimmy Carter, and he was treated with the deepest levels of respect by all White House staff. Presidents included.

"My pleasure, sir," replied the neatly dressed steward as he walked out the left-hand side of the Oval Office. A moment later, there was a knock at the other door to the right, which led to the President's personal secretary's office.

Without a response from the President, the door opened, and the other members of the tight-five walked in.

"Please, sit down," President Lang said to them as he pointed to the two sofas that faced each other in the middle of the room, enveloping the coffee table where the glasses of scotch sat.

"Help yourself," he said to his trusted companions as he took a seat in a cushioned wooden chair in front of the world-famous Resolute desk.

A deep orange glow flooded the room, the result of the sun setting over a hazy Washington sky. The smell of freshly placed flowers mixed with the aroma of the recently vacuumed floors. Despite an international emergency unfolding, domestic duties in the presidential office still continued.

President Lang took a sip from his glass, before focusing on business.

"Okay, Anna, what have you got up your sleeve?" asked the President.

"Sir, Director Blake's team has done brilliantly to identify the island where the cyber-attack occurred," she began.

"Agreed," responded the President enthusiastically, nodding his head whilst raising his glass in the direction of the NSA Director. "Though I'm sure Brad and I would have preferred if it had never happened in the first place," he said, firmly this time, suggesting his initial response was made tongue-in-cheek.

She could tell the President wanted the solutions he had asked for, so she decided to dispense with any of the platitudes and preambles.

"Yes, sir. Apart from the location of the island, we've also uncovered that the attack occurred because a code was inserted into the cyber network on Air Force One, which enabled a full navigation and electronics system shut down at a specific location during your flight."

The President almost dropped his glass.

"What?" he said.

"NSA analysts have discovered that a code was deliberately placed into the network onboard in order to facilitate a remote cyber-attack while the plane was flying in the vicinity of the island, Zulu One, in the South China Sea," briefed Director Dawn.

She leaned forward in her seat and opened her folder, pulling out an A4 paper map of the region where the cyber-attack occurred. The President also leaned forward in his chair.

The Director pointed to the island, and then to a small 'x' which marked where Air Force One was located when the hack occurred. The President looked closely and listened intensely.

"But that's miles from the island," he said.

"Yes, sir. However, the hackers were able to leverage off of a military satellite to infiltrate the network's system. The code embedded was designed to expose the network to an attack. The code opened up the firewalls, and then the hackers remotely inserted the virus that shut down the systems, forcing the diversion to Dili."

The President looked at Secretary Kingston in shock.

"How the hell could that happen?" asked the Secretary.

The two uniformed military officers in the room looked at each other seriously, then both at Director Dawn.

She took a sip from her glass, then inhaled deeply. She didn't cherish having to tell the President what she was about to. She looked up at him.

"Sir, Air Force One was sabotaged. It was done by a person or persons with access to the highly sensitive and classified systems both in the NSA and on the plane," she said succinctly.

President Lang looked at her in disbelief. He then glanced over at the others who, apart from the Secretary, had obviously already been informed.

He stood up and moved to his desk, where he gently placed down his glass. He walked over to the window, placing his hands on his hips and looking out into the famous Rose Garden and up at the orange coloured sky.

The room sat in silence for a moment.

The President composed himself and returned to the group.

"So, we've got a traitor in our midst. Does that rule the Chinese out?"

"No, sir, not at all," said Admiral Pike. "This occurred from an island that, from all available intelligence, at very least has a Chinese presence."

"Along with that, sir," added Director Blake, "we can't be certain that we haven't been infiltrated by Chinese or other state entities that, possibly with the support of a traitor or traitors, have gained access to highly classified U.S. cyber intellectual property that allowed the attack to occur."

"Is the entire country at risk?" asked the President.

"No, sir. We're currently conducting a full audit and check on all national-level systems," said Director Blake. "Everything from the electrical grids to the nuclear arsenal. In terms of cyber-hacking, this was specific and targeted."

The President didn't look convinced.

"Conducting an attack on anything larger would have raised many red-flags and have been identified earlier, even if undertaken by someone on the inside. We're confident the protocols in place are still adequate," said Director Blake.

The President looked again at the A4 map.

"Why conduct a remote attack?" he asked.

"I'm sorry, sir?" asked Director Blake, unsure about the question.

The President looked up, remaining calm and thinking analytically and clearly, despite his tiredness.

"Why attack Air Force One remotely? Why not just embed a code that would make the plane crash? It seems rather complicated the way they did it."

"The code simply opened up the firewalls onboard, exposing the network to a remote hack, which in turn forced the diversion to Dili. The networks would have been able to detect any malicious coding that was trying to make the plane crash, so it would have been impossible to place a virus into the network. Therefore, the code that was embedded was inserted via a friendly system and looked completely innocuous. The systems don't account for treasonous activity by our own people," said Director Blake.

The President just shook his head and sighed.

"My God," he said.

"I survive nearly one-hundred sorties over Iraq, and then I nearly get killed on what is supposedly the safest plane in the world. I think I'm going to throw up," said the Secretary, taking in most of his glass of scotch in one gulp.

"We don't think the location of the diversion was a coincidence, either," added Director Dawn.

"How so?" asked the Secretary.

"Simply, because there were men with Stinger missiles waiting for the plane when you tried to make an emergency landing in Dili. Apart from not being able to embed malicious code onto the onboard network, one of the benefits, from an attacker's point of view, of shooting the plane down instead of just making it crash is that they would have been able to film the whole thing. That's indicative of terrorist tradecraft. It would be a massive psychological win for whatever perverted cause they believe in."

"*If* it was terrorism," observed the President.

"Umm, yes, sir," replied the Director.

The President took a large sip from his own glass, before thinking for a moment.

"So, whoever was involved knew about the protocols of emergency landings, too," pointed out the President, his analytical mind coming to the fore.

"Indeed," replied the CIA Director.

"Okay. What now?" he asked.

"Sir, the computer networks have been completely removed and replaced on the entire presidential fleet. Now that we know what to look for, it won't happen again," Director Blake said, trying to sound reassuring.

"Alright. Now, how do we get back the initiative? Because right now I feel like we're swinging in the wind, and the American people want action. The financial markets are treading water – barely; and the rest of the world is scared that the two largest economies are possibly going to war," summarised the President.

"Sir," began the CIA Director, "the narrative your administration is setting at the moment is that this was a despicable act that the U.S. will not allow to go unpunished. However, even amongst ourselves in this room, we can't agree on who to blame."

"What *do* you agree on?" asked President Lang, sitting forward in his chair and looking around at each of them.

"Firstly, that more intelligence is needed, and that the most likely source of that is on that island named Zulu One. Our thinking is that the complexities we've seen involved mean that a nation-state had to have sponsored this and that China is the most likely culprit."

Director Dawn looked over to Admiral Pike, who opened up his leather folder and removed a large envelope. He handed it to the CIA Director, who removed a few sheets and images from within.

'Top Secret' was stamped at the top of the folder in thick red ink.

"Sir, we request your approval to conduct a clandestine operation onto Zulu One with the view of determining who and what is on that island," she said to the President.

President Lang exhaled deeply.

"Wow, Anna. You want to infiltrate what may well be a Chinese military base?"

"Essentially, sir – Yes," she replied. "There is no official sovereign ownership of this island at this point. It's disputed amongst several nations all claiming ownership of the myriad of islands in the Spratly group and around the southern part of the South China Sea."

"I'm not sure the Chinese will see it that way," said the Secretary, "it seems they've already set up shop there, even if they do deny it. How do you propose to get around that?"

The Director already had an answer.

"JSOC has been working on developing plans to conduct infiltration onto the islands within the contested area, in order to conduct reconnaissance and direct action in the event of war," she said, referring to the U.S. Joint Special Operations Command – the military group responsible for conducting highly sensitive special operations globally.

This was the group that had planned and executed the raid against Osama bin Laden's compound in Pakistan.

The President sifted through some of the notes and images that were being presented to him.

"We can't find out more any other way?" he asked.

"Human intelligence and actual eyes on a target are still the best method, sir. We believe tapping their communications may help us find out who was responsible internally for sabotaging Air Force One, too," she said.

"How would it work?"

The CIA Director looked up at Admiral Pike.

"Sir, with your approval, we'd like to enact 'Plan Poseidon'. This operation would see a small team of about half a dozen special forces and intelligence operatives inserted clandestinely from a submarine and onto Zulu One. They will conduct a reconnaissance of the island to gain more fidelity of the military assets on there to help determine who owns them. We'll also seek to tap their electronics and signals equipment to help identify who they're communicating with."

"What units would be involved?" asked President Lang.

"The plan calls for these teams to be formed based on mission requirements. Considering the short timeframe that we've got available, we'd use some of the assets we've already got available in that area. The plan allows for the use of allied special forces from the region. We've currently got a small combined U.S./Australian element ready which was forward postured on Guam after the attack in Dili."

The President looked at the Admiral, almost bemused.

"Okay, so what's the issue?"

"The Australian who stopped the attack in Dili, we'd like to use him as part of the mission. He's currently part of the team that has provided us the most intelligence so far. Because Australia's an allied nation and we'd like to use their personnel, we will need to —"

The President nodded and raised his hand, cutting off the Admiral. He stood up from his seat and walked over to his desk. He pressed a button on the intercom which was connected to his secretary's desk outside.

"Helen, I need the Australian Prime Minister, now please," he politely asked.

"Right away, sir," came the voice back through the metallic box on his desk.

The President returned to his seat.

"I'll ask the Prime Minister, but I don't think the Aussies will say no," he said as he sat down.

"Thank you, sir," said the Admiral.

"What will the timeframe be?" asked the Secretary.

"On the President's order, we'll consolidate the team in place on Guam. From there they'll be inserted onto a U.S. submarine in the vicinity of the South China Sea, which will then move to a position close to the island. The team will then make a maritime insertion onto Zulu One. We expect we can have them on the island in just over thirty-six hours," briefed the Admiral.

The President raised his eyebrows.

"That quick?" he asked.

"Yes, sir. JSOC units plan and prepare for these types of operations frequently. This deployment will actually be outside our usual timeframe metrics. We're only delayed here because we need to insert them by submarine, and that needs to be performed very carefully."

Although he had never served in uniform himself, President Lang held the utmost respect for the armed forces, and he had been elected on a platform that he would ensure the U.S. maintained a military capable of supporting and defending American interests globally.

There was a knock on the door, and almost immediately it opened up.

The President's personal secretary stuck her head around the door.

"The Australian Prime Minister on line one, sir," she said.

President Lang nodded, stood up from his chair and moved to his desk.

He picked up the receiver and placed it to his ear, before pressing a single button on the secured phone that now linked him directly to Canberra.

"Ed – It's Jack Lang. We need your help."

The President spoke to the Australian Prime Minister for several minutes. They had a good relationship, not only because the two nations had deep historical ties, but also because the two men personally got on very well.

Once finished, the President returned to his seat. He looked straight at his staff with an air of complete focus.

"Okay, I want whatever arseholes who tried to blow us up in a U.S. federal prison ASAP. Keep looking."

"Sir, Plan Poseidon?" asked the Admiral, looking hopefully at his Commander-in-Chief.

The President looked over the notes and images one last time. He looked around the room for any dissenting faces.

There were none.

He drank the remaining scotch from his glass, and then looked authoritatively over at his most senior military officer.

"Approved."

10

The C-130 J-model U.S. Air Force Hercules transport plane taxied along the tarmac at Anderson Air Force base on Guam as the sun began to set over in the west. The young pilot watched as the airman waving two light wands guided him to the stop point. He skilfully manoeuvred the plane to a halt just inches short of the intended target.

The loadmasters wasted no time in lowering the rear door, and the plane's two lone passengers disembarked, carrying black tactical backpacks in their hands.

Zach Kryton rubbed his eyes as they adjusted to the light. The warm humid air once again hit his face, having only briefly being interrupted by the air-conditioning on the plane. He and Clay Dalton had made the most of the opportunity to get some rest during their flight from the CIA Black Site.

The roar of the engines powering down made it difficult to communicate, so they moved away from the plane and its rotating propellers.

The base was a hive of activity. A B-1 bomber taxied down the runway, preparing for a mission to an unknown location. Several B-52 heavy bombers were parked in their slots on the tarmac, as well as a few C-17 Globemaster heavy transport planes.

'Welcome to Andersen Airfield' read the old looking sign above the passenger terminal. A U.S. flag fluttered in the light breeze. The base had been modernised in recent years as part of U.S. re-engagement in the Pacific, but there were still rusty old remnants of World War Two lying around beyond the perimeter fence on the edge of the runway.

The smell of jet fuel and freshly cut grass wafted through the air.

A lone figure standing by a Humvee waved to them in front of the passenger gates. Kryton gently tapped the American on his good shoulder. His arm and upper chest were still bandaged up. Although he wouldn't be able to take part in any operations, Clay Dalton's planning skills would still be invaluable.

The two operators walked over to where Cav was standing. His trademark aviator sunglasses adorned his face. He wore an Australian Army camouflage uniform. A low-visibility Australian flag was velcroed to his upper left sleeve.

"Are those glasses as per ASOD's?" asked Kryton jokingly as the two men shook hands, Kryton using the acronym to describe the *Army Standards of Dress* manual – the guide for the proper wearing of uniforms in the Australian Army, inclusive of sunglasses.

The conventional army dictated some fairly strict uniform protocols, which was often viewed as 'more of a suggestion' by the special forces.

"Buggered if I know?" replied Cav with a big smile. "Good to see you, mate."

He reached out and took Dalton's bag off of him.

"And how are you, Frogman?" he asked the Texan as they shook hands.

"I hate those noisy planes," he replied, still trying to pop his ears.

Cav laughed.

The three moved towards the Humvee.

"How are you feeling?"

"Getting there – a bit of rehab ahead; but all said and done, I'm just grateful to be here," said Dalton.

"Well, lucky you had someone there to save you," said Cav, winking at the American whose life he had saved a week earlier.

"Yeah – terrible bedside manner, though," retorted Dalton jokingly.

Dalton jumped into the back while Kryton joined Cav in the front.

They wasted no time getting down to business.

"Who've we got with us?" asked Kryton as Cav placed the Humvee into gear and started driving off of the tarmac.

"You and me to begin with," said Cav. "Two guys from Sydney, and one of Dalton's guys from SEAL Team Three."

Australian special forces often referred to themselves by their unit's home location – Sydney being the home base of the 2nd Commando Regiment.

"And the sixth guy?" asked Dalton, knowing that Colonel Lamar had briefed them that it would be a six-man operation before they left the Black Site.

"A cyber operator from the CIA. He's ex-U.S. Special Forces and from all accounts a solid operator."

Cav drove along the road that ran parallel to the runway. Another B-1 bomber took off into the sunset, its engines roaring as it sought to gain altitude.

"How long have you been here for?" Kryton asked Cav.

"Not long over forty-eight hours. We received orders about five hours ago so we're well into the planning cycle. We'll brief you in and finish the planning. Two hours of rehearsals, then kit check, and we're wheels up at midnight."

"Flight time?" asked Dalton.

"The air force pilot says five hours. We'll fly normal height for the majority of the run-in, then hit the deck just west of the Philippines to get under potential Chinese radar. We'll jump in with the SDV and get picked up by the submarine," said Cav, referring to the SEAL Delivery Vehicle – essentially a motorised underwater taxi that ferries special forces operators across the ocean.

They continued driving for another five minutes until they reached a secluded set of buildings to the south of the runway. It was surrounded by a large fence and two U.S. Air Force security guards stood armed at the front gate.

They waved the three men through.

Cav drove into an industrial-size warehouse and parked to the side of a set of Humvees.

It looked like an old fisheries warehouse, and it smelt like one too.

An improvised Special Operations Command and Control Element – SOCCE – had been established in the middle of the warehouse. This was essentially the nerve centre and would be where the operation would be run from. A set of boards with various maps and classified images had been set up and formed into a U-shape, with a large table in the middle.

An eclectic mix of intelligence and military personnel were operating computers and secured phones out of deployable hard-case boxes. This temporary SOCCE had been in place for only a few days, established almost immediately after the attack on Air Force One in anticipation of such a mission.

The three men jumped out of the Humvee and walked over to where four other men were standing.

"You know Macca and Ando," said Cav to Kryton.

"Holy crap!" exclaimed Kryton enthusiastically, shaking the hands of the two Australian commandos who would be part of the team. They would be the sniper pair.

"Haven't seen you since I carried you to the hospital in Kabul," joked Ando.

"Well it was an IED – and I recall you telling me to just 'walk it off'," said Kryton.

They all laughed, remembering the last time they had worked together conducting special operations in Afghanistan.

Cav introduced Dalton to the sniper pair also.

He then turned to face the two other two men at the table.

"Zac Kryton, Clay Dalton – meet Matt James of SEAL Team Three, and Rob Fox of somewhere in the CIA so discreet I've never heard of it," said Cav in typical Australian humour.

The men shook hands as Fox looked at Cav while shaking his head in faux-disdain.

"I'm the cyber guy," said Fox simply.

Dalton looked at James curiously.

"You were on BUD/S a class or two behind me, weren't you?" the Texan asked his fellow SEAL.

"Sure was, I arrived at the Teams after you started your time with the Aussies. The boys back home were glad to hear you're doing okay," said James, pointing to Dalton's arm and shoulder.

"It'll heal. But I will sit this one out none the less," laughed Dalton.

Introductions and pleasantries aside, Cav guided the team, now complete as one, over to the table where a map of the area of operations was laid out, as well as a few recent satellite images of Zulu One.

"Okay, our callsign is 'Poseidon One'. Zach is team leader as this is an intelligence and reconnaissance mission," commenced Cav. "I'll be 2IC. While as operators we know it's not ideal to put a small team, unproven together, like this at such short notice, the fact is both our militaries are being worked overtime, we've all got similar training and this mission calls for some unique skillsets – and since they couldn't find anyone else, they called us!" joked Cav at the unusual situation.

The team nodded and smiled before Cav continued.

"We'll conduct a PLF with the SDV at rendezvous point 'Alpha' just before dawn," he said, pointing to a spot on the map in the middle of the ocean near the base of the South China Sea.

A Parachute Load Follow – or PLF – was a means of inserting both men and equipment into the water, usually some distance from the intended target or next to a submarine or ship.

Cav then traced his finger on the map and moved it to another point further north, about fifteen kilometres from point Alpha.

"The submarine *Delaware* will pick us up out of the water and once onboard with the kit stowed, we'll conduct a submerged transit throughout the day to drop-off point Bravo. From here we'll move into the SDV and infiltrate while submerged to the southern part of Zulu One, cache the SDV in the littorals, then once ashore we'll move our way to this point here, called Charlie," he briefed, pointing to an elevated rocky outlet overlooking the harbour inlet.

"Our primary mission is to observe activity on the island, gaining as much intelligence as possible. Particular focus will be on these communications towers located here," he said pointing to an array of towers and antennas near a rectangular building, about one-hundred metres from the wharf.

The sniper pair pulled out their small planning companions – beige covered notebooks with various rulers, markers and notepads inside.

"Ando and Macca will set up an overwatch position at Charlie. Kryton and Fox will wait until the cover of darkness and move down to the communications tower and enter it. James and I will tag along in support. From there, Fox will do whatever magic he does to tap into their communications."

"Voodoo magic," said Fox, winking at Kryton.

"If you can get me cheap Wi-Fi, you can do whatever you want," replied Kryton.

Fox laughed. He warmed to the Australians immediately.

"Seriously, my intent is to place a trace into their software by tapping into their communications transmissions boxes. Chinese software security is about preventing wireless and remote access. They won't expect someone going straight in through the hard-line. If we're successful, we'll then be able to track all historical and future communications from that facility, as well as all of the devices its ever communicated with," the cyber expert briefed them.

"Sounds like we're doing to them what was done to us," observed Dalton.

"Pretty much. From here, NSA should be able to narrow down from where and by whom the attack on Air Force One occurred. At very least, we'll prove whether or not the Chinese were directly behind it."

"Phew – we've come a long way since Tetris," observed Cav.

"How long will you need?" asked Kryton.

"I've practiced this back at Langley and on the flights over here. If all goes well, no more than five minutes."

Kryton nodded while looking over the maps and images.

"Exfil?" asked Dalton. "I don't want to be stuck here by myself with no-one to play cards with."

Cav pointed back to the map.

"We'll return to the cached SDV's before sunrise the next morning, then back out to the sub. Total mission time from wheels up here to back on the submarine is thirty-five hours."

"Macca and I have secured comms transmission ability, so we can send both images, voice and text data across an encrypted satellite straight back to the Pacific Command Headquarters in Pearl Harbour, who will get it to the strategic agencies," added Ando.

"If it hasn't been hacked?" queried Cav sarcastically.

Ando laughed.

"JOC assures us it's secure – so we'll have to hope. Otherwise, the Chinese may get a very detailed position of our location," said the sniper.

They all glanced at each other, seeking further questions or input.

The sound of a massive C-17 Globemaster taking off from the runway echoed throughout the warehouse.

"Okay, time check," said Kryton. "It's now 2000 hours. We'll split off into our pairs and continue planning. Back here for a final brief in one hour. We'll do weapons and comms check, and also rehearsals for the movement on the island. Wheels up at midnight. Questions?"

There were none from the team.

A noisy clang came from the other side of the warehouse as a support staff member from the U.S. Navy dropped a spanner onto the back of a flatbed truck. The sailors were packing the SDV for the parachute drop.

"Well I have one," said Kryton, looking at Dalton and James who had just started a small conversation on the side.

The SEALs looked over at the Australian, who had a confused look on his face.

"Anyone able to tell us Aussies how the hell we operate that?"

James and Dalton smiled.

"Come on," said James, "I'll show you."

11

A dull red light permeated through the control room. The radioman listened closely on the designated frequency; static came through his headphone, disturbed intermittently due to the waves lapping up against the extended mast sticking out above the waterline, not far above the console where he was sitting, but separated by a thick steel casing.

The Virginia class submarine USS *Delaware* was transiting through the water at periscope depth, moving quietly at a little over six knots. With its radio mast fully extended, the on-duty radioman listened for the approaching Globemaster.

"Anything?" asked Lieutenant-Commander Hackett, the Executive Officer – or XO – of the *Delaware*.

"No, sir. Still listening," replied the young radioman.

The XO looked over at the Officer-of-the-Deck.

"We're definitely in position?" he asked curiously.

"Yes, sir," replied the junior ensign, looking at his chart.

The young radioman placed his hand against his ear, subconsciously trying to improve the sound coming through the headphone.

He turned slightly to look at the XO and shook his head softly.

Sitting nearby in the Captain's chair was the Commanding Officer – or CO – Captain Daniels. A veteran CO who had completed numerous patrols throughout his distinguished career, he was one of the most experienced submarine commanders in the U.S. Navy.

The veteran officer appeared calm as he sat upright in his chair. If he had any misgivings, they weren't obvious.

Submarine commanders never liked transiting on or near the surface, especially in potentially hostile waters. That's not what submarines were designed for.

The radioman turned sharply back to face his console.

62

"Sir, Poseidon One is inbound and requests confirmatory acknowledgement," said the radioman loudly to ensure the officers had heard and understood the communication that had just been received from the inbound Globemaster.

Daniels jumped up from his chair and moved with haste to the centre of the control room.

"Up periscope," he said as he squatted down to help manoeuvre the periscope into a position that would allow him to see immediately everything that was happening on the surface.

He placed his eyes over the two circular rubber pieces. The red light illuminating the control room ensured that his night vision would be working as he looked through the glass casing that reflected the images from above the waterline down into the submarine.

Daniels flicked a switch on the handle that helped him twist the periscope in a 360-degree direction. Another switch allowed the infra-red function to work. He was now looking through the periscope with its night-vision engaged.

"Tell Poseidon One to go to IR," ordered Daniels.

The radioman spoke quietly into the mouthpiece that was connected to his headphones.

Daniels looked patiently through the periscope. It was focused to the east, the expected direction of the inbound U.S. Air Force plane. He could see several stars on what was obviously a very clear night. An eerie green and black glow filled his vision.

"Surface contacts?" he asked to the navigator's yeoman.

"None, sir. Scope is clear," replied the young female sailor who was diligently observing her console for any ships or boats that could compromise their position.

This particular spot had been chosen for the parachute drop because it was away from known shipping routes, but that didn't mean that an errant drug runner or a lost fishing crew wouldn't get in the way and compromise the whole thing.

The CO squinted, looking for an outline or a shape indicating the arrival of his guests.

A moment later, the flicker of a strobe light, albeit at a distance, could be seen over the horizon.

Daniels smiled softly.

"Tell Poseidon One we acknowledge their IR signal and their approach," he instructed to the radioman.

The CO lowered the periscope and returned to his chair.

"Officer-of-the-Deck, surface the ship," he ordered.

"Surface the ship. Aye, sir," came the reply from the ensign.

An electric buzz went through the control room. Daniels had trained his crew well, and their drills were flawless. He wanted to ensure they weren't on the surface for a minute longer than they needed to be.

A young sailor passed the CO a waterproof jacket. Daniels, along with the XO and the sailor who would act as a lookout, moved to a vertical ladder. They would observe the pick-up from the roof of the conning tower utilising NVGs – Night Vision Goggles.

The submarine would have no lights on at any time whilst on the surface.

A few kilometres away up in the sky at approximately fifteen-hundred feet, Zach Kryton hunched down between two U.S. Air Force pilots in the cockpit of the Globemaster. He placed some headphones over his ears so that he could talk to the pilots through the intercom without having to shout over the roar of the turbine engines.

"You called for me," he said.

"Sir, out there at one o'clock," said the co-pilot, handing him a set of NVG enabled binoculars.

Kryton placed them over his eyes. He looked to where the co-pilot was pointing down at the water. Through the green and black glow, he could clearly see a line of disturbed water. He followed it up until he could see the outline of a surfaced submarine moving slowly through the ocean.

He smiled slightly.

It was a great effort by the pilots to have successfully navigated to what was a relatively tiny spot in the middle of open water – and to also find a previously submerged submarine no less.

Kryton handed back the binoculars to the co-pilot.

"We'll do a flyover for the final descent and then make the approach head-on. Green light in five minutes," the pilot informed Kryton.

The Australian operator gave the thumbs up, then moved down the stairs of the cockpit and returned to the cargo hold at the rear of the plane.

He walked down to the tail where his team was sitting, fully kitted up in all of their parachuting gear and awaiting their final orders.

Kryton gave the thumbs up to Cav, then held his palm up with all five fingers extended. Cav returned both hand signals – it indicated that they would jump in five minutes.

Cav, as a qualified parachute jumpmaster, would control the movements from here on.

The team stood up and made a single file on the left-hand side of the plane. To their right was the large and well-packed load that was the SDV. Their equipment was contained within, so they would be jumping in what was known as clean skin. Their drysuits would enable them to stay warm. A set of fins was strapped to each man, which they would place over their feet once in the water.

The operators steadied themselves as the massive plane made some sharp turns, the pilots turning to get onto the path that would fly them directly next to the submarine at one-thousand feet.

They each connected a metallic hook fastened to a thick detachable strap to a steel cable that ran the length of the plane. This would be a static line jump, meaning that once they exited the plane and started falling to the earth, the detachable strap would pull the parachute from the packs now tightly fastened to their back. The airflow created by the short free-fall would then rush into the parachute as it unfurled from the pack, and form a canopy which would allow the men to fall safely to the water below.

The red light that had to this point protected their night vision was turned off, and the plane was plunged into relative darkness.

But only for a moment.

The rear door of the large plane was lowered, exposing the dark void that was the night sky. A gush of cold air came flying in and enveloped everyone onboard. Although the moon had descended for the evening, there was still an ambient glow being provided by the stars that were still shining. Kryton stood behind Cav, who was at the front of the line of men. He could see a faint line in the distance. It was the horizon, barely distinguishing the sky from the water.

The air force loadmasters made a final check of the SDV, which had its own set of parachutes. It was sitting on a flatbed on a set of rails and would be electronically rolled out of the rear of the plane.

The six operators would follow, seeking to stay close enough together to ensure they remained as minimally spread apart as possible when in the water, but far enough apart to allow each of their parachutes the space to open properly, which would reduce the likelihood that they would collide while in the sky.

Parachuting itself was an inherently risky activity – but even more so when done at night.

The loadmaster stood in front of Cav. His headpiece was connected to a cable that was plugged into the plane's internal communications. He would be talking to the pilot directly, who would be issuing the countdown.

The loadmaster said something into Cav's ear.

Cav turned around and with his free hand held up a single finger.

"One minute," he shouted.

Each man reciprocated, holding up a single finger and repeating the words. In their other hand they firmly held the strap to their parachute, ensuring it wouldn't accidentally get caught up on the myriad of buckles and hooks that protruded from their safety harnesses which held the packs of their parachutes.

They stepped forward slightly, each man going through his own mental steps in order to steel himself for the jump ahead.

Even though each man had made numerous training and combat jumps throughout their careers, each one brought with it an equal amount of dread and excitement. All parachutists hated the anticipation. They just wanted to get out of the plane and get the nervousness over with. This one particularly so, considering the mission they had ahead of them.

"Stand by," shouted the loadmaster, stepping to the side to allow a clear path for the SDV and the six-man team to exit the plane.

Each man watched intensely at the small red light in front of them on the frame of the plane. The pilots steadied their controls, seeking to make the jump as smooth as possible.

The co-pilot's finger hovered over a small red button in the middle console in the cockpit.

The pilot sitting next to him looked out of the windscreen to the water below. At just the right moment, he spoke to his co-pilot.

"Go," he said into the intercom.

The co-pilot pressed the button.

At the rear of the plane, the previously red light turned a welcoming bright green.

The loadmasters released the SDV payload, which suddenly dropped off of the rear of the plane and into the darkness.

The six operators ran after it, following the man in front of him and letting go of the straps that they had held in their hands as they literally stepped off of the edge of the tail of the plane, letting gravity do its job.

Kryton followed Cav out.

The rush of wind hit his face like a bucket of cold water. His heart jumped into his mouth as he experienced the initial free-fall that accompanied the first few moments of the jump. The roar of the four turbine engines combined with the wind to create a sound that mimicked a freeway during peak hour traffic.

One-thousand, two-thousand, three-thousand, he shouted in his head, performing the count which gave his parachute the time required to draw the air needed to form a canopy. If it hadn't unfurled after these few seconds, then he would have only moments to pull the hook to inflate his reserve parachute, which sat in a separate pack on the front of his body.

He looked up and observed the large round shape that was his canopy.

So far, so good.

He looked around. There was now almost a deathly silence, with only the increasingly faint sound of the Globemaster flying off into the distance. For a moment, he let himself enjoy the view, falling softly as a very slight breeze forced him to drift down at a slight angle. He could see the other canopies, staggered across the sky. Below him and to his left, and seemingly getting bigger, was the shape of the submarine now motionless in the water.

Kryton estimated that he would land less than one-hundred metres from it. He pulled on the cords above his head which helped to guide the direction of his descent.

Not a bad effort from the pilots, he thought to himself.

Up on the conning tower of the *Delaware*, the CO looked skyward to observe the descending operators.

The SDV landed first, just off of the stern of the submarine. The operators then landed in an orderly fashion in quick succession.

"Recovery crew, recover the package," he softly instructed into his intercom.

Almost ten minutes later to the second, all six operators had been recovered, and the SDV had been properly secured to the submarine, with all connections locked in to prepare for its use many hours from now.

Daniels returned down to the control room and removed the waterproof jacket he had been wearing while aloft. He sat down in his Captain's chair and watched as the young sailor who had acted as the lookout descended the vertical ladder, having closed the watertight hatch behind him.

"Submarine secure, sir," said the young sailor.

"Officer-of-the-Deck, submerge the ship," ordered the CO.

"Submerge the ship. Aye, sir," diligently replied the ensign.

Fifteen minutes later, the *Delaware* was transiting submerged through the water at eight knots.

Its payload safely aboard.

Its destination was now north.

12

The six operators spread out across the darkened beach. They carefully and tactfully moved up the gentle slope, leaving the cold ocean behind them and heading towards the relative protection of the tree line less than forty metres away.

They moved in complete silence. The sounds of the waves hitting the beach masked the crunching noise of the leaves and broken twigs under their feet. Kryton placed his left hand up to his side – the signal to come to a halt. Each operator was wearing NVGs and immediately stopped upon seeing the signal. They all took a knee, the rear two operators facing back down the way they came, ensuring they had at least one team member looking in each direction for any threats.

They continued to stay silent, their chests heaving as they breathed in heavily – the result of the physical exertion required of the swim ashore after they had cached the SDV.

They had rehearsed the basic movement techniques back on Guam.

They would stay in position in complete silence for the next twenty minutes, allowing their senses to acclimatise to the new surroundings.

The small semi-tropical island was alive as a cacophony of buzzing insects and nocturnal animals scavenging amongst the foliage filled the night sky. Wildlife can detect foreign movement, sounds and smells in their environment, and will often go quiet until they've ascertained the potential threat. This lack of noise can betray the location of a small force seeking to infiltrate an enemy's position, so the noise was most welcoming to the team.

Kryton looked at his wrist, illuminated by the green and black light of his NVG.

The waterproof G-Shock brand watch read out the time.

It was a little after 2130.

He looked around and gathered his thoughts. They were on schedule, and so far it appeared there was no compromise. He turned his watch over to expose the small circular compass attached to the wrist band. They had studied the maps and images closely as part of the planning. Kryton had a mental navigational map in his head, and they would be able to walk to point Charlie using just a watch and the compass.

He anticipated it would take the team approximately two hours to reach their intended destination. He reached down to press on the 'talk' switch of his radio.

"Comms check," he said softly, wanting to do another radio check before stepping off to commence the walk.

"Cav."

"Ando."

"Macca."

"James."

"Fox."

Each operator replied softly in turn – their respective radios proven to be working. Although they had this technology, they would conduct as much movement and communication as possible using hand signals, or at very most through soft whispering. The radios would be saved for when the team needed to break up, and was essentially a communication measure of last resort.

Kryton took a deep breath and waited.

After he was happy the right amount of time had passed and he was confident they were able to proceed, he turned around to face the sniper pair who were crouched down by a tree. Once he had Ando's attention, he gave a pre-determined hand signal, indicating that he wanted Ando to pass the message back to the SOCCE on Guam that they were on the island safely.

Ando acknowledged this instruction and sent a coded message through the satellite back to Guam. The staff at the SOCCE would be tracking their every move.

Once he had received a confirmatory message back from the SOCCE, he gave the thumbs up to Kryton.

Cav moved up to join his friend.

They crouched next to each other, and Cav placed his mouth next to Kryton's ear.

"All good?" he whispered softly.

Kryton nodded. He looked at his friend. They all wore disruptive patterned uniforms of their respective nations, now wet from the swim ashore. Their faces were covered in camouflage cream. NVGs covered their eyes.

"Cache the fins here, we move out in two minutes," Kryton instructed.

Cav gave a thumbs up, then stood up to move to each team member. They would cache their fins until they needed them again to swim back out to the SDV.

Two minutes later, Kryton stood up, extended his hand by his side and waved it up in a raising motion.

The operators began their walk to point Charlie.

13

A little over two hours later, the six men arrived at their destination. A small rocky ledge, protected by leafy foliage, provided the perfect location to observe down onto the inlet where the small group of huts and the wharf was located.

The move had been slow and methodical, not only for tactical purposes but to ensure that none of them fell over while traversing the unfamiliar and unstable terrain.

While trained to deal with such an incident, an injured operator would seriously compromise the mission, so every appropriate precaution needed to be taken.

Kryton crouched down on the ledge. It was solid rock, and straddled a small culvert which was covered with dense foliage.

They couldn't have found a better spot. The other men took positions nearby, staying in pairs.

They looked down over the inlet. It was about a kilometre from their current position. About halfway between the culvert and the huts, the trees and scrub opened up into flat grass, which appeared to be about knee height.

Cav moved into a spot next to Kryton.

"See that?" Kryton whispered.

Cav looked down onto the inlet. A small smile appeared on his face.

"Submarine!" he replied softly.

The intelligence from the keyhole satellites showed a submarine in position two days ago, but they didn't expect it to still be there. They would be able to gather intelligence on it, and hopefully trace its recent activity.

Kryton lifted his NVGs – he wanted to look down on the wharf to see how much artificial light was down there. It would help give an indication of the presence of people.

A few scattered lights softly illuminated the exterior of the few huts, which were huddled together in a small group opposite the wharf.

Kryton counted five in total, with a few smaller storage sheds and shipping containers sporadically spread within its vicinity.

A man-made breakwater jutted out of the inlet, providing some protection to the small wharf from the elements of the open ocean. The concrete wharf had several light poles evenly spaced along its length, which would have been less than two-hundred metres long.

The sound of a diesel generator was audible, its noise carried to the team's position by a light breeze. There was no apparent movement they could see.

"Fox, join me," Kryton said softly into his radio.

A moment later, the cyber expert hunched down next to Kryton.

"What have we got?" he asked softly.

Kryton had been looking through a small pair of binoculars. He handed them to Fox.

"Down there, to the right of the wharf and under the big antenna," Kryton said.

The American placed the binoculars to his eyes and looked down to the small facility. He followed Kryton's directions until he could see a cubicle just to the side of the communications array.

"Is that it, per the satellite photos?" asked Kryton.

Fox nodded.

The American fiddled with a few items in his backpack. He ensured the lock picking equipment was at the top, as well as the tablet he would use to hack into the communications network.

The sniper pair moved into a position that would give them not only observation of the facility, but enough cover and concealment so they could observe undetected from any wandering souls. Intelligence had indicated that the island was otherwise uninhabited – but intelligence could often be wrong.

As planned back on Guam, they waited for thirty minutes, allowing enough time to make initial observations of the facility, but also to rest for a short while. They took a moment to each take in some water and a small amount of food. It had been over eight hours since they had detached from the *Delaware* in the SDV and made their way ashore, and they had physically exerted themselves extensively in that time.

Kryton removed his NVGs for a moment and looked at his watch.

It was almost midnight.

He looked over at the magnificent vista in front of him, slightly illuminated by starlight. The sounds of the nocturnal wildlife filled the air, and although the temperature had dropped, it was still warmer on the ledge now that their clothes had dried out than it had been in the ocean a few hours earlier.

Twenty minutes later, Kryton radioed Ando and Macca who had moved to a higher part of the ledge to set up their sniper hide.

"Ando – good to go?" he asked.

Typically, special forces operators who had worked closely together over periods of time used codenames, usually based on their role or specialisation. Being such a small and multi-skilled team, they had decided to do away with such requirements.

"We're in position, ready to cover you," came the reply.

Kryton placed his suppressed M-4 carbine down by his side, removed his gloves and rubbed his hands.

Despite all they had done and achieved over the past twenty-four hours, this phase they were about to embark on was the difficult part.

Kryton looked around. He could see that the other three operators that would go down to the facility with him were ready.

He thought for a moment about the past two weeks. Less than a fortnight ago he was teaching at the Royal Military College back in Canberra, and now here he was leading a special operations element into something very dangerous and completely unknown.

He wouldn't trade it for anything in the world.

He exhaled deeply. The swim and walk had tested him.

More cardio between jobs next time, he thought to himself.

He placed the NVGs back over his eyes and waited for a moment for his eyes to readjust to the eerie glow.

"Okay, let's go," he whispered into his radio.

The team stood up one by one and started softly moving down the hill, trying to use the foliage and tree line as best as possible to conceal their movement. Kryton took the lead, followed by Cav, Fox, and then James.

Ando and Macca remained in their hide. Their powerful spotter scopes would allow them to see advanced signs of danger, and they would be able to warn the team to any imminent threats.

14

The four-man team made good time as they slowly approached their target. The occasional sound of a wild pig snorting echoed amongst the otherwise indistinguishable noises being made by the insects and other nocturnal wildlife.

"At least two tangos appear to be conducting a casual patrol around the sub," came the updated report from Macca across the team's radio network.

They would all be able to hear the updates being provided by the sniper pair.

'Tangos' was the term they would use for any otherwise unidentified personnel observed. They were, for all intents and purposes, in hostile territory.

Two hours later, they reached the knee-high grass. They crouched low near the edge of the tree line and waited for a few minutes. Once again, they had already rehearsed their next movements back on Guam, so they didn't need to say a word.

Cav, Fox, and James would simply wait for Kryton's signal.

Kryton softly pressed on his radio transmission button five times. This was the signal to the sniper pair that they were now about to start their final approach through the grass. Even a whisper at this point could risk being heard from any guards that the facility might have had in place. Up until now, the sniper role had been to make observations and update the approaching team. From now on, however, they would have to be prepared to engage a target in case of any contact with any threats.

They would do all that they could to avoid any kinetic engagement, in order to avoid any compromise that might result in mission failure.

The operation had been personally directed by the White House, so success was expected.

A well-defined three clicks came back through Kryton's earpiece, indicating that the sniper pair had heard and understood.

The four operators were about four-hundred metres away from the closest building. Apart from the lights by the wharf, the far side of the facility was covered in relative darkness.

Cav moved up next to Kryton.

He gave a sly questioning nod, seeking to confirm their previously arranged plans.

Kryton gave a thumbs up.

He turned to look at Fox. Their goal now was to reach the transmission box and place the tap. He pointed at the American cyber specialist, then placed his hand on his head – the signal for Fox to join him.

The CIA operative did so, and without a word they stood up slightly and commenced their move, crouched like tigers, through the grass and to the box.

Cav and James followed, separated by no more than thirty metres.

The four of them moved slowly. The outline of the infrastructure became clearer as they approached. The distinct smell of diesel fuel and seaweed became more predominant as they got closer to the wharf area, as did the smell of cooking rice.

At the planned spot, Cav and James parted ways and moved to their designated positions on the edge of the closest building. They looked around the top of the rooves, looking for any cameras that might compromise their position.

There were none.

Fortunately, the lights at the facility were focused around the submarine, and only a few very dull lights were above the entrance to the huts, struggling to provide any decent illumination.

They were like the old fibro buildings used on various Pacific islands by the Japanese in the Second World War to house soldiers and equipment, and appeared to be very old and unkempt. Kryton and Fox crouched next to each other in the grass and observed their target location. The transmission box was unprotected, and the towers didn't have a bright flashing aircraft warning light above it that most transmission towers are required to have.

Kryton thought that it might be an old base that had only recently been occupied. The lack of a fluttering Chinese flag, which flew at all Chinese military installations, even a fuel dump, started to make him think that this wasn't an actual Chinese military facility.

Those questions and theories would have to wait.

After a few minutes, Fox placed his hand on Kryton's right shoulder and squeezed.

The signal to go.

Kryton remained crouched down and started moving at a steady pace towards the transmission box. His M-4 was raised in line with his eyesight, scanning his front for potential threats.

In less than a minute, the two men reached their target and kneeled by the side of the box. They removed their NVGs – the ambient light from the facility was enough to see, and the lack of decent depth perception that the illuminating technology provided would make it hard for Fox to do his work.

Kryton focused forward in the direction of the wharf, his weapon still raised in anticipation of possible compromise. There were two huts facing the wharf, which had what looked like a jeep parked in front of the far one. He could see two Chinese men casually pacing the wharf, about ninety metres from where he was hiding.

The two pacing men each had an SKS assault rifle slung over their shoulder, one of them smoking as they loudly conversed in what Kryton assessed to be Mandarin. The light breeze was carrying sound away towards the breakwater, a blessing for the two-man team seeking to break into a metallic box.

The fact one of the Chinese men was smoking next to a submarine that had barrels of diesel next to it on the wharf made Kryton question their professionalism.

While Kryton applied cover, Fox removed a lock-picking set from one of the pouches on his backpack and in less than a minute, he had successfully removed the flimsy lock. The plan was to make it look like they had never been there, not to leave a trail of destruction.

Fox had hoped the box would be poorly protected, but he was still surprised at the relative lack of security. It was obvious that the current tenants were not expecting any visitors on the island.

He opened the door slowly, trying to avoid the tinny screeching that comes with opening a rusty door. Fox looked at the several racks of hardware inside, multiple cables coming out of them and running up a central pipe in the roof of the box, all leading into the base of the tower they were now crouching under.

The CIA operative took out a tablet and a USB cable, and like an IT technician, simply placed his cable into one of the black boxes that had small operational lights flickering at the front of them.

Fox moved as close to the box as he could, using his floppy jungle operations hat to conceal the dull glow that his tablet was emitting.

Kryton kept scanning his horizon. A seagull out on a night mission landed a few feet in front of him and looked at the Australian curiously.

No chips for you here, Kryton thought to himself.

The mangy looking bird walked around for a little bit, ruffled up its feathers, then flew off towards the submarine, where several of its colleagues sat on the conning tower.

He turned to look at Fox, who was furiously tapping on the tablet. It felt like it was taking a lifetime, but in reality, it had been only two minutes. He took some comfort from knowing that Cav and James were inconspicuously hidden nearby, ready to provide fire support in the event of a compromise.

"How long?" he whispered to Fox.

"Almost, their firewalls are tougher than I thought."

There was nothing Kryton could do but wait.

Suddenly, a loud noise came from the far hut. Three figures walked out, talking loudly but inaudibly. Kryton focused his weapon on the three men. The scope on his rifle enhanced the image, but he could only see the outlines of three men. Two carried rifles over their shoulders, the third was larger and seemed to have a pistol holstered onto his belt.

"Three tangos in front of the far hut," came the update from the sniper hide.

Kryton and Fox remained perfectly still.

The three unknown men kept chatting loudly. A moment later another two came out with what appeared to be a large wooden box. They placed it on the back of the jeep, then went inside the hut only to come outside a moment later to repeat the process.

The same two men then climbed into the jeep and drove off up the wharf to the submarine. The other three men stayed standing outside the front of the hut.

"I'm taking images," came the voice of Cav over the radio.

Cav was positioned further away, and his small digital surveillance camera was designed to not make any sound or give off any light or reflection. Perfect for this type of task.

Kryton looked at Fox. He motioned with his hand to keep going.

Fox furiously tapped away at the tablet for another minute, before running a connection check.

They would have to wait for another two minutes while the sniper pair waited for the NSA operators in the SOCCE on Guam to send through the message that the tap had worked.

They continued to wait.

The light breeze picked up just a little, but it was enough to carry the sound of the conversation of the men at the jeep.

Kryton listened closely, trying to make out what they were saying. Something said by one of the men had caught his attention.

He looked at Fox, who had obviously heard the same thing.

American? he silently mouthed to his companion.

Fox nodded slightly. The conversation was mostly indistinguishable, but the accent was clear enough.

Kryton raised his rifle again to look through his scope.

Walk into the light, he thought to himself, trying to will the men to move closer to the illumination of the hut so he could get a better image.

"Good transmission received. We're live and broadcasting," said Macca across the radio, reporting that Fox's hack had been successful.

Fox looked at the Australian and gave the thumbs up. Kryton nodded, but they weren't done yet. He wanted to know about the American accent.

He monkey-crawled the few metres over to Fox.

"We need to get closer to recon that hut," he whispered so softly that it was barely audible.

Fox nodded, returned his cyber equipment to his backpack and placed it over his shoulders. Kryton looked around to the rear of the closest small shed, then quickly moved off into the relative darkness, Fox right behind him. The two men moved along the rear of the huts, scanning their front for threats and slowing making their way towards the hut where the three men had been seen. There was no light at the rear of the huts, but the light from the wharf softly illuminated the space in between them, so the operators had to dart across the open space, no more than seven or eight metres, one at a time.

Kryton could hear Macca on the radio, briefing Cav and James as to the other team member's movements.

"Careful, mate," Macca said quietly into the mouthpiece of his radio.

Once they had made it to the end hut, they found that it was raised slightly off of the ground. Kryton got down onto his stomach, followed by Fox.

Like two snakes seeking their prey, they manoeuvred their way under the hut until they reached a point where they could see the three men more clearly.

The jeep had returned, but the other two men were nowhere to be seen.

Kryton and Fox were less than twenty metres away from the small group, huddled around in a group and talking.

The two with the SKS rifles were ethnically Chinese, but the third man was clearly Caucasian.

He could hear them talking, mostly just idle chatter. Kryton could hear the patter of footsteps on the floorboards above him, moving towards the front of the hut. A mesh door burst open and a set of feet moved rapidly down the stairs and over to where the men were standing.

Kryton removed his own small camera from his webbing, manipulated a few buttons and started recording. The Caucasian man had turned, but his face was now being blocked by one of the Chinese men.

Move you little bastard, thought Kryton.

He was in a terribly uncomfortable position, but that wasn't important now.

"The boxes are loaded, sir," came a Chinese accent speaking English from one of the men in front of Kryton.

"Good. We sail at dawn," replied an American accent – the man Kryton was struggling to get an image of.

"Yes, sir," came the reply.

Kryton was still filming.

Just one picture, he thought to himself.

The man blocking his view stood still for a moment, speaking in Mandarin to the other two Chinese men.

He turned around and quickly moved inside, exposing the front of the Caucasian man.

Just under six-foot-tall, reasonably well built, clean-shaven and with dark short length hair, the man was wearing the 'operator' uniform – khaki pants, a button-up tactical shirt with its sleeves rolled up, and olive-green boots.

He looked like a mercenary.

"Finalise the documents, then join me on the submarine," he instructed to the two Chinese men, before turning and climbing into the jeep and driving up the wharf.

The other two men ran inside the hut.

Kryton turned around on his stomach, and slowly crawled over to where Fox had been lying flat on his stomach, silent the entire time. He raised his index finger and made a small circling motion – the signal for a rendezvous. It meant they had got what they had come for, and it was time to go back.

Fox made his way out from under the hut first, followed by Kryton. The Australian placed his free hand on the American's shoulder and squeezed. Fox darted across the dimly lit gap between the huts, then crouched low once he reached the other side. Kryton was about to move across himself when the sniper's voice spoke in his earpiece.

"Zach, freeze," the calm voice said over the radio.

Kryton had to force himself back to stop the momentum he had started generating in his move forward. He crouched behind the hut in the darkness.

He could hear several voices. A small group of Chinese men appeared from outside of another one of the huts. Macca had seen them exit and had observed them walking across the face of the huts. If Kryton had stepped out to follow Fox, he would likely have been compromised.

One of the intruders was kicking a cylindrical metal container, and shouting at it in Mandarin. Two of his friends were behind him, laughing. They appeared drunk.

Kryton got as low to the ground as he could. There was a small crack in the edge of the hut he was hiding behind, and he could see the commotion from his hidden position.

The two laughing men moved slightly into the space between the huts where Kryton and Fox were both now hiding and dropped to their haunches. One pulled out a cigarette pack, offered one to his companion, who accepted, then lit both with a lighter. The third man returned to the hut.

It took only a few moments for the noxious smell of thick Middle-Eastern tobacco to waft to their position. Kryton knew the smell well, he had spent many hours sitting in circles with Iraqi elders seeking information, drinking diesel-like coffee and smoking similar smelling cigarettes.

He often wondered how it was that he didn't already have lung cancer.

A few moments later, the other Chinese man returned, carrying a box that he placed down next to the other two. They all reached inside and took out the contents. A small boiler, three mugs and a small container with leaves in it

It was a tea set.

One of the men set up the boiler while the others prepared the tea.

It was now obvious that the metal container that they had been kicking was a water boiler, and that somehow it had broken. The men were improvising in order to make their tea.

Kryton had no idea who these men were or why they were rummaging around making tea in the middle of the night – none of that mattered at the moment.

He looked over at Fox, who was crouched down behind the next hut. He could see the faint outline of his face. Fox rolled his eyes.

They couldn't be compromised, so simply engaging the men was not an option.

"I count nine tangos," said Macca across the radio.

That was another reason. They were outnumbered and the team was separated. There was absolutely nothing they could do but wait.

And wait they did.

All six operators, each on their own patch of turf on this insect riddled island in the middle of nowhere.

Like owls in the night.

Waiting. Observing.

Their special forces training being tested. The patience and discipline to stay in complete silence being called upon.

James and Cav were in their own positions, rifles ready to engage if needed.

The minutes quickly turned into an hour. And then another, and another.

The Chinese men sat there in a little circle, occasionally joined by one or two others as they swapped out their submarine patrol duties on every hour.

Kryton looked up at the sky. The stars had all but disappeared. To the east, he could see a faint purple glow. The impending morning twilight was approaching like an out of control freight train.

Their fears of compromise were rightly exacerbated by the approaching dawn. The dark of the night afforded their current protection, but even morning daylight would leave them fully exposed, making it virtually impossible to get back to the tree line without being seen.

The jeep came screeching back into the area in front of the hut, with the Caucasian man jumping out and screaming.

"Let's go, let's go. Fucking move. They're here," he shouted in English.

A loud bell started ringing, indicating some kind of alarm.

The Chinese men who were sitting making tea jumped up, knocking over the boiler and their small chairs. The doors of the two huts that Kryton and Fox were hiding behind came flying open. Several more men, also with SKS rifles, came flying out and started running around in a disorganised manner.

Kryton looked at Fox. His heart jumped a beat. Fox returned the gaze, a sense of fear in his eyes. They thought they had been compromised.

They readied themselves for engagement. Both men simultaneously removed the safety catches from their rifles.

But there was no gunfire. None of the men came their way.

Kryton gently poked his head out from behind the hut.

What was going on?

Had they been compromised?

Why was no-one firing at them?

He looked back over at Fox, who had a similar confused look on his face.

Cav and James, also in concealed positions that risked compromise with the approaching dawn, steeled themselves for a fight.

"Something's going on, but I don't think it's you guys," Macca said through the radio. "They're running towards the sub; it looks like they're trying to get ready to sail. Oh…holy shit."

Kryton and Fox heard it before Macca could explain what he had seen.

Two large thumps well off to the north-west echoed over the sound of the ringing bell.

A whistling noise drew closer, piercing the sky.

Kryton had just enough time to look at Fox and could see that the American also knew exactly what the approaching sound was. They both hit the deck as hard as they could as the first two explosions shook the ground they were lying on.

One artillery shell had landed near the submarine, another in front of one of the small sheds near where they knew Cav was hiding.

"Two naval ships, north-west and closing on the island," Macca blurted through the radio as bits of rock and dirt fell around the two operators lying behind the huts.

The sniper pair had been so focused on covering the four men down near the inlet that they hadn't observed the silhouette of two grey vessels approaching from over the horizon.

"Are they ours?" asked Kryton, his face still flush to the ground, hoping that they might be able to call off the bombardment while friendly forces were in the area.

"Unsure, wait one," replied Macca.

The commando removed a small set of binoculars from his pack and stood up from where he had been lying next to Ando. He placed them over his eyes and squinted, trying to adjust the lenses in order to get a clear picture. Through the lenses, he could see the clear outline of the warships. Macca watched helplessly as he looked at the distinct red and yellow flag of China fluttered from the masts of the two ships.

"Oh, shit –" he muttered under his breath before jumping back down on the ground.

"Chinese. They're Chinese. Get the fuck out of there."

Two more thumps emanated from the distance as the second round of volleys from the Chinese warships were fired at their targets.

Kryton and Fox hit the ground again, praying that the shells would land as far away from their position as possible.

The two shells landed harmlessly in the water in the vicinity of the submarine.

Kryton jumped up and ran to where Fox was trying to get up. The threat of getting blown into the sky far outweighed the threat of compromise. They could at least fight other men with guns.

"Cav, James, we're coming to you. Acknowledge," Kryton said into his radio.

"Copy," said James.

"Cav?" asked Kryton.

Nothing.

"Cav?" he said again, as he and Fox started moving along the rear of the huts, crouched down with their weapons raised.

The first rays of the sun were now starting to appear over the horizon. The whole area was now well-lit, and there was nowhere to hide.

"He's down. Come to us," James said over the radio.

Fuck, thought Kryton as he and Fox raced to the location of the other two operators.

They raced in between the huts and towards the smaller set of sheds.

Two Chinese men came around, running and looking confused. Kryton saw them first, raised his rifle and fired four bullets. Two for each man in the upper chest. Fox stayed on his tail, covering the rear as they continued to move tactfully through the facility and towards their colleagues. They scanned their arcs as they moved forward, professionally covering the full 360-degrees around them.

'Slow is smooth. Smooth is fast.'

The mantra used by special operators the world over, meaning that performing the drills correctly and methodically was more effective than rushing them and making potentially lethal mistakes.

The two men reached the corner of a small storage shed. Kryton looked around and saw James kneeling next to a prone body in a small culvert next to what appeared to be a dirt road.

"We're coming in from behind you," Kryton informed James through the radio.

Fox jumped out from behind the shed first, facing down towards the wharf where all the commotion was taking place. He covered Kryton, who jumped out from behind the shed and ran for about ten metres. The Australian then stopped, turned, took a knee facing the wharf and raised his rifle to cover Fox.

"GO," he shouted to Fox as two more Chinese shells landed, one exploding in a large fireball the hut that Kryton had been hiding behind only moments earlier. Bits of wood and dirt rained down across the facility.

Fox stood up, turned around from his position, ran back past Kryton and then once again took a knee facing up the way from where he had just come.

The process known as 'pepper-potting'.

The two operators repeated this until they had joined up with James and Cav.

Fox took a knee, firing his rifle at a Chinese man who had stumbled out from one of the small sheds, dropping him like a fly. Two other Chinese men, confused by all the commotion, started firing indiscriminately.

Their position was in the open and incredibly exposed.

"Behind the shed over there," Kryton motioned to James as the two well-trained operators grabbed Cav under his armpits and dragged his body to where there was better cover.

Fox then joined them.

Two bullets ricocheted above the head of the kneeling cyber expert, who returned fire at the obviously confused Chinese man who had fired them with his SKS rifle.

"They have no idea what's going on," observed Fox as he fired several more bullets in the direction of the wharf.

"Cav? Cav?" said Kryton, slapping the face of his old friend whom they had leaned up against the wall of the shed.

There was no blood or obvious signs of damage.

Kryton reached into a pocket in the sleeve of his camouflaged shirt and pulled out a small tube. He placed it under the nose of the unconscious commando.

Cav coughed, then quickly tried to stand up. James held him down while he regained his senses.

"You okay?" asked Kryton.

"What happened?"

Kryton let out a relieved sigh.

"You got knocked out," he said to his friend.

"Zach, over here," interrupted Fox who was still providing cover at the corner of the wall.

Kryton moved over to Fox while James gave Cav a quick once over, bringing him back up to speed as to what was happening.

Several more shells landed across the facility.

As Kryton kneeled next to Fox, one shell hit what appeared to be an oil dump near the breakwater. A deafening explosion roared across the island as several barrels were launched into the air, returning to earth in a trail of thick black smoke, forcing the men near the wharf to run for their lives, and in some cases jump into the water.

The two operators watched as one of the barrels seemingly floated down from the sky, landing with a dull splash next to the sub.

"It's just like Donkey Kong," said Fox, almost mesmerised by the scene unfolding in front of them.

Men ran everywhere, diving for cover and firing wildly at shadows, still obviously unsure of what was happening.

Kryton could see the submarine had moved away from its berth. The Caucasian man with the American accent was standing on the conning tower, screaming at some men who were pulling in ropes that had tied the submarine to the wharf.

Thick black smoke was filling the sky. The acrid smell of diesel wafted over the whole area.

It was obvious the submarine was trying to make a break for it.

The lack of further explosions suggested that the shelling had stopped, but the noise of alarm bells, burning buildings and screaming men dying in pain still filled the air.

"Macca, what can you see?" Kryton asked over the radio.

"It looks like they're putting some boats into the water from the ships. I think they might be trying to put troops ashore," replied Macca.

Kryton and Fox observed as the submarine started making way to the edge of the inlet.

"That smoke is pretty thick, I reckon they think they've hit the sub," Macca said from his position on the rocky ledge.

Kryton looked at the billowing smoke not far from where he was. The dark plumes would help give the submarine the cover it needed to make an escape.

Kryton went back to Cav and James.

"You okay?" he asked his friend.

Cav nodded as James poured some water over the groggy man's face to help rouse him.

"Good, because we have to go. There's Chinese troops coming this way, and we haven't got tickets to this show," Kryton said.

Cav sat up a little taller, shook the water from his head and nodded.

"We're coming back to you now. Send a sit-rep to *Delaware*," Kryton said to the sniper pair over the radio, instructing them to send a situation report to their ride home.

"Roger. Standing by."

"Fox," said Kryton, calling the American back from where he was giving the rest of the team cover with his rifle.

Fox joined the other three and together they started moving hurriedly in single file towards the tree line and away from the engagement zone.

15

They reached the tree line without incident and quickly started to ascend the foothills back up to the sniper pair, much quicker than they had conducted the walk-in earlier that night.

They walked so fast that they were almost in a light jog.

They had to get out of that area and back down to the beach.

Kryton turned around to look back across the facility.

He watched as the submarine sail into the open ocean. It rapidly submerged, leaving a small trail of bubbling, disturbed water in its wake. Somehow it had miraculously escaped the Chinese naval bombardment.

He looked over at Cav.

"You good?" he asked.

"Yeah, just one hell of a headache."

They continued their move back up the hill.

Kryton's legs ached as he led the team back up towards the sniper pair.

His mind raced.

Why would Chinese ships attack their own people?

Who was the Caucasian man?

The intelligence analyst in him was trying to piece the puzzle together.

He was now certain that this was some sort of terrorist or mercenary group – and a very well organised one. Apart from some of the drug cartels in South America, no other known non-nation state organisation had access to submarines. And even the ones the cartels had were of very poor design and often sank.

Less than an hour later, the team reformed as a complete unit on the rocky ledge. They looked down at the smoking mess that was the facility they had just been at.

"The tower's still intact," observed Fox.

"At least we managed to do what we came for," noted Cav, rubbing his head.

He handed his small camera to Macca. Kryton did likewise. The sniper pair would transmit the images via satellite to the SOCCE on Guam, along with further updates as to the happenings on the island.

James pulled out a small torch and moved Cav to a shaded area away from the ledge. He shone it in Cav's eyes several times, checking for pupil dilation.

"I don't think you're concussed, but we had better get you looked at anyway."

The others stayed in their concealed positions and watched as several Chinese Navy inflatable boats entered the inlet while a helicopter flew overhead of the wharf.

Kryton watched as troops poured out of the boats, running through the facility and detaining the few remaining people who were there.

"Chinese Marines," stated Kryton as he looked through the binoculars, observing their distinct grey uniforms.

He scanned across the horizon through the remaining smoke to the west to look at the two Chinese destroyers which had very nearly blown him off of the island.

"And they would be Type 052 destroyers. They look brand new," he added.

Fox moved to sit down next to Kryton. He was breathing heavily, just like the other three who had just rapidly walked up the hill.

"What now?"

"We need to get off of this island. I imagine they'll conduct a clearance of it soon. We don't want to be caught here," said Kryton. "Once we're back on *Delaware,* we can talk to the SOCCE and try to work out what the hell is going on."

"About that," said Macca cautiously.

Kryton looked over at him. He didn't like the look on his face.

"What?"

"*Delaware* has detached from our mission and has been tasked to follow the Chinese sub," Macca informed them.

Kryton looked around at his team.

James was shaking his head.

"Sounds about right."

Kryton sighed.

"Oh well," he said. "Plan B."

He looked at his watch. It was nearly 0900 hours. The sun was now well and truly up in the sky, occasionally obscured by a few clouds. The temperature was rising fast, bringing the humidity with it.

"I thought Plan B was to stay in this location until we could get picked up," said Fox.

"We can't stay here," said Kryton. "So, Plan B is whatever gets us out of here."

"There's an Australian Navy task group to the south of here. We're directed to drive the SDV out and rendezvous with them," briefed Macca.

The team all just looked at each other. They started giggling.

Special operations demanded that its people maintained an ability to adapt to rapidly changing and demanding environments. They were trained for just such events.

It didn't mean that the situation didn't suck, though.

"Why would they attack their own facility?" asked Fox, replicating the thoughts and questions Kryton had already formed in his own mind.

"No idea. But I think it's safe to say that the attack on your President wasn't done by the Chinese government. This has to be something asymmetric. Something not being done by a country."

He looked at Macca.

"Have you sent the images and the sit-rep?"

"Guam's received it," replied Macca.

"Good. That American guy is of interest to me. We need to see what we can find out about him."

"Yanks. Always with their hand in it one way or another," said Cav sarcastically while looking at his U.S. counterparts.

"At least *we* didn't get blown up," replied James, tapping his finger on his own head.

Cav just smiled in his defeat at the banter. His head hurt like hell.

Levity helped ease stressful situations and could help numb the pain that would have to be endured until they could get off of the island and to safety.

They looked down at the smouldering facility. The helicopter appeared to be doing ferry runs from one of the destroyers to the area near the wharf.

The snipers packed up their equipment and stood up, ready to move out.

Kryton looked at each man. They were tired, but ready. Like the professionals they were.

"Okay, boys. Let's go swimming."

16

The thick rubber of the front tyres of the helicopter touched the flight deck just milliseconds apart. The pilot pushed forward on the collective to place downward pressure on the rotors, forcing the big metal beast to stay on the sightly pitching ship.

Two sailors ran from the side of the superstructure and placed chocks under the wheels, preventing any further movement and helping the helicopter to stay in place.

A skilfully executed landing by the young naval pilot.

The six operators climbed down from the back of the MH-60R Seahawk helicopter and onto the flight deck of Her Majesty's Australian Ship *Hobart*.

A recently commissioned Aegis capable air-warfare destroyer, *Hobart* was leading a small Australian task force that included the frigates HMAS *Parramatta* and HMAS *Anzac*.

They made their way into the internals of the ship, placing their gear down onto a wooden table at the rear of the flight hangar. Two sailors brought them some food and water, as well as some dry clothes. The intelligence personnel had wasted no time, and were ready and waiting with notepads to ask questions.

The SDV had been cached on the seabed, and if the situation permitted, would be recovered at a later date. The team had then been picked up by the helicopter, winched from in the middle of the ocean.

A navy doctor appeared with another sailor, a medic, who would look over Cav for any internal injuries sustained from the Chinese naval bombardment.

"Are you here to collect your poker winnings?" asked the doctor.

Kryton looked at the doctor, before smiling and extending his hand.

Lieutenant Jim Giles was an old acquaintance of Kryton's. The operator had introduced the doctor to a young lady, who later became his wife, at some party so long ago they both were unlikely to remember the purpose of it.

"Cav – meet Jig," said Kryton.

Cav shook the doctor's hand while the medic took his blood pressure.

"Why Jig?" asked Cav bluntly, curious at what was obviously a nickname.

The naval doctor took a small torch and shone it in Cav's eyes, checking for pupil dilation and other signs of potential concussion.

"Well, although I still deny it, apparently I once decided to do a little dance on a taxi in Kings Cross one night after a drinking session with this one," he informed Cav while motioning with his head at Kryton.

"The name stuck!"

Cav thought for second and then smiled.

"Ahhh. Like Irish jig. Nice."

The doctor looked over Cav, sticking a light into his ears and getting the seated operator to do a few reflex exercises. Kryton stood by watching, hoping that nothing was too seriously wrong with his friend.

"Well, you'll be fine. We'll get some fluids into you and monitor you over the next few hours. Some rest would help too," said the doctor.

"Thanks, mate," replied Cav, shaking the lieutenant's hand.

Cav jumped up and went to join his teammates who were unpacking their equipment and answering the questions of the intelligence staff.

Kryton walked with Jig to the middle of the hangar, sharing some small talk and quickly catching up.

"The CO wants to see you on the bridge, ASAP," Jig informed Kryton. "You know where to find it?"

"Well, it's my first time on this class of ship, but I'm sure I'll find my way."

He pointed over to his team.

"Can you give those guys a once over? We've had a long few days."

The doctor nodded.

"We'll have a brew in the wardroom later," said Jig before walking with his medic to where the rest of the team was standing.

Kryton quickly changed into a dry camouflage uniform, before grabbing a bread roll from the plate provided by the sailors and commencing his walk up to the long, narrow passageways of the ship and towards where he knew the bridge would likely be.

The hum of the generators permeated throughout the passageways. Kryton found the ship to be in pristine condition, reflective of a well-disciplined crew.

After a few minutes and several sets of stairs later, Kryton made his way to the open door at the rear of the bridge. It was a hive of activity. The lookouts with binoculars were keeping watch over the open ocean, while the officers and signallers engaged in animated conversation as they communicated with the accompanying ships.

Kryton was familiar with naval protocol, so he waited until he got the attention of one of the boatswain mates on watch before coming onto the bridge proper. A young, heavily bearded sailor saw him waiting at the door.

"Captain, sir. You have a guest," said the sailor to the man sitting upright in the comfortable looking chair to the side of the bridge.

The CO looked over his shoulder and towards Kryton. He waved the operator over.

"Sergeant Kryton, sir," said the operator, introducing himself to the commander of the ship.

"I'm Mitchell. Welcome aboard," said Commander Scott Mitchell, shaking Kryton's hand.

A stocky man in his mid-forties, Mitchell had joined the Royal Australian Navy later in life, but had ascended through the ranks through skill and sheer hard work. He was well respected by his crew.

"You blokes must be bloody important for us to take such a risk to come near this part of the world," said the CO, seemingly in a friendly manner but with a hint of pointed seriousness about it.

"Well, we appreciate you coming to get us, sir," said Kryton respectfully. He appreciated these were contested waters, but he expected nothing less from the navy.

The CO returned his gaze out through the window of the bridge. One of the frigates passed ahead of the *Hobart's* bow, taking a position to the port side of the destroyer.

The task force was sailing south-east, seeking to remove itself from the area where Chinese vessels were starting to appear not far over the horizon.

Their job was to observe happenings and to support any U.S. action – not to go looking for a fight.

The phone next to the CO's chair rang. The commander picked it up and had a short conversation with someone on the other end. Once finished, he placed the receiver down.

"We're going to move closer to the Filipino coastline," said the CO while looking out the window through a pair of binoculars. "We've got orders to get you ashore as soon as possible."

"Orders? From whom?" asked Kryton.

The CO jumped down from his elevated chair.

"Officer-of-the-Watch, I'll be in the ops room," he said.

"Aye, sir," came the reply from the young female officer who was controlling the activity on the bridge.

Commander Mitchell looked up at Kryton.

"Follow me, someone wants to talk to you."

17

Kryton followed the CO down a set of stairs and along one of the many passageways. Situated below the bridge was the operations room – the ops room for short.

The ship's captain opened the door and walked in, Kryton followed close behind and closed the door. The CO pulled back a curtain and stepped into the ops room proper.

A dull eerie blue glow illuminated the room. Several sailors were sitting at the myriad of consoles, each conducting various duties including monitoring the sea, surface and sub-surface space around the task force. Numerous television screens covered the walls; some showed CCTV vision of the flight deck and the forecastle of the ship, others had television broadcasts being beamed in via satellite. The main screen in the middle of the wall displayed the threat picture. Blue icons displayed the location of friendly ships and aircraft, while red icons displayed known Chinese positions.

"The *Delaware* was detached to chase the Chinese sub you encountered on the island. They're having trouble, though, as the Chinese also seem to be trying to find it," said the CO to Kryton.

"What is its direction?" asked Kryton.

"Last known position was close to the coastline and heading north. We think that it's trying to use the shore to confuse sonar," said the CO.

"Can you maintain tracking?" asked Kryton.

"It's hard as there's lots of disturbance in that area due to the number of reefs and because tracking a sub while hiding from other ships is hard work. I'm sure the *Delaware* will be able to keep on its tail. They've been instructed to trail it and find out where it's going."

The CO pulled Kryton closer to the wall to allow the intelligence sailors who had been talking to his team space to get back into the ops room.

"Being an older diesel-electric sub, it needs to snorkel near the surface every so often to change out its air. Apparently, the Americans are now tracking communications from the sub. It seems your mission was successful enough."

Kryton nodded, closely looking at the threat picture on the screen before him.

There were still so many unanswered questions, but at least they now had a lead.

"Why not just sink it?" he asked the CO.

Commander Mitchell chuckled. He guided Kryton over to the side of the ops room where a table with several charts were laid out.

"Orders are to follow it only. Your friends in Canberra can explain as to the reasons why," he said.

One of the intelligence sailors spoke to the CO.

"Sir, the encrypted video conference is ready for Sergeant Kryton."

The CO nodded.

"I'll leave you to it, I have to get back up to the bridge," said the CO. "Don't worry. We'll take good care of your team."

"Thanks, sir," said Kryton. He appreciated the commander's hospitality.

Kryton looked back at the sailor.

"Over here, Sarge," said the young sailor.

He guided Kryton to a small, secluded office where a laptop computer had been set up.

"They're ready for you. Headphones are on the seat," said the sailor, before he walked off to return to his duties.

Kryton assumed he was about to talk to the SOCCE back on Guam. He sat down and placed the headphones over his ears. He tapped on the spacebar to activate the call.

Two familiar faces appeared on the screen.

"Jesus, you look like hell," came the Australian voice through the earpiece.

It caught Kryton by surprise. He laughed.

"Good to see you too, Jonas," he said sarcastically. "I thought that the service had been cut out of this," he said, referring to Australia's foreign intelligence agency, the Australian Secret Intelligence Service – ASIS.

It was Jonas on the screen. Sitting next to him was Jo. They were huddled around their own computer at some office in the suburbs of Canberra where the ASIS headquarters was located.

"Well, initially. But it turns out the President wanted us involved, particularly yourself. The U.S. are stretched very thin globally, so they need all the allies they can get at the moment."

Kryton nodded. He looked across the screen over to Jo. His throat suddenly felt dry. He took a shallow breath.

"Well, guess you now know why I haven't bought you that coffee yet," he said, referring to the promise he had made to her when he last saw her in Dili.

He hated having to obfuscate the truth to her, but he thought she would understand.

She just shook her head and let out a knowing smile.

"It's all good. I hear you've been getting to play soldier again."

Kryton leaned back and smiled.

"Yeah, it's been fun. Jumping into shark-infested waters and getting my ears blown out by Chinese gunfire. Can't believe I gave all that up," he said.

He took a bite from the bread roll and took a sip from the bottle of water the sailor had placed on the table for him. The ease with which both went down made him realise that he hadn't eaten in nearly two full days.

"But I'm good for my promise," he added.

She smiled and gave the thumbs up.

He leaned forward in the chair, seeking to focus on the issue at hand.

"I thought this was now a military operation. How are you guys involved?"

Jonas pulled out a manila folder and opened it.

"This is an intelligence-led operation now," he said. "Look on the screen and I'll send some images."

Kryton chewed on the bread as Jonas began to give his brief.

"Your mission on the island was successful in that we've been able to answer some of the technical questions outstanding from the attack on Air Force One," he commenced.

"Glad to have been able to help," said Kryton.

Jonas continued.

"The tower on the island is definitely where the remote hack into Air Force One took place from. The NSA believes that they have a double-agent on the inside who facilitated the sabotage of the plane using some sort of advanced coding which was embedded into the plane. That allowed them to hack in from the island while the plane was flying within the area."

Shit, thought Kryton to himself, leaning back in his chair and running his hands through his hair.

Jo continued the brief.

"We're working with the CIA closely here, it's now a combined operation. We've analysed the information your team managed to send back from the island."

A file with a picture appeared on the screen. Kryton's eyes widened in recognition.

"That's the guy I saw on the island," he said assuredly. "Who is he?"

"His name is Peter Wallis. Formerly of the NSA's highly secretive 'denied-access' team. These guys are essentially special operations for the NSA. They go and tap wires and listen to conversations in the worst places," said Jo.

Kryton looked closely at the image in front of him. The overall intelligence picture was becoming clearer. Now they had a name and a face.

"The Americans want him. He's now unofficially the world's most wanted man," continued Jo as she and Jonas appeared back on the screen.

"Unofficially?"

"They're keeping it all pretty close hold. They're unsure who else might be involved within the NSA, or even at government level. That's why they're keen to have us involved in this. A known ally without a compromise. The Australian Signals Directorate is taking the lead on most of the signals and cyber analysis. There's still lots of data to go through."

"So that's why they can't sink the sub, they want him alive," Kryton mumbled to himself.

"He's highly trained and apparently went off of the grid several months ago. Colleagues said his demeanour had changed, and he was saying all sorts of anti-government things," added Jonas.

"Hmm, okay. What else do we know?"

"The tower has stopped transmitting, but that's to be expected since the Chinese Navy is now on the island, and whoever was operating there is either dead or on the rogue sub. The CIA Director is briefing the President as we speak, and they're now suggesting a narrative that the attack was *not* Chinese sponsored," said Jo.

"What other evidence have we got to support that?" asked Kryton.

"Your cyber expert's tap into the tower was able to extrapolate lots of data from internet and phone communications. A lot has been matched to the phones and information you obtained in Dili and from the detainee you interrogated at the CIA Black Site," said Jonas.

"It appears your Iranian detainee was telling the truth. He's only a low-level mercenary recruited over the dark web with a few others from the Middle-East, one of whom you killed in Dili," said Jo.

Kryton took a notebook from his pocket and made a few notes. His mind was racing with information, but it was all starting to come together. He inhaled deeply, grateful that it appeared that a potential regional conflict between superpowers would not be happening after all.

Hopefully.

"What are the Chinese doing? They're obviously aware of something, otherwise, they wouldn't have tried to blow up an island," he asked.

"The U.S. is using back-channels to talk to them. A lot of political rhetoric has come from both sides in the past two weeks, and although it seems like they aren't involved, it pays to err on the side of caution. We'll be seeking to help find out what they know first, and perhaps from there build a common picture of the situation," said Jonas.

"So, what now?" asked Kryton.

"Fortunately, we've been able to get a whole range of new phones and communication channels from the island tower that we can now track. We've identified a link between a phone we believe is getting used by Wallis on the submarine to one in Taiwan. We think the sub is heading there now."

Kryton nodded while rubbing the increasingly thick stubble on his chin. He suddenly felt sorry for the sailors in the ops room who were no doubt breathing in his foul odour.

"Has Taiwan been informed?" asked Kryton.

"No. The U.S. will track the sub's movements. They want to find out who's on the other end of the phone," added Jonas.

"Additionally," exclaimed Jo, "through cyber analysis we've traced financial transactions linked to Wallis on the dark web to a Chinese armaments company based in Hong Kong. We're not sure who they are yet but we're looking into it."

Kryton looked up to see Cav peering through the curtain and into the small office. He could only guess as to how Cav had managed to weasel his way into the heavily restricted ops room.

He placed his hand up as if to say *just a moment*, before looking back at the screen.

"You'll be transported to Manila and then onwards to Taipei," said Jonas. "Well make contact with you once there and brief you on your task. The naval intelligence officer onboard will brief you as to the movements."

Kryton found it hard to conceal a smile.

"You up for it?" asked Jo.

While he loved jumping out of planes and dragging his arse through the jungle, it was the intelligence game that he loved best.

High risk, discreet and covert. Classic spy stuff.

"You bet," he said simply.

"Good luck," said Jonas.

"See you soon," added Jo.

Kryton waved at the screen, before signing off from the call.

He sat back in the chair and thought for a moment. They now had a name, a possible location, yet not a reason. That could come later. For now, his focus was on getting to Taipei.

He walked out of the small office and over to where Cav was trying to flirt with a very disinterested young female sailor who was trying to write up a report.

He placed his arm around his mates' shoulder, guiding him out of the ops room.

"Come on, you need to rest. Doctor's orders," he said to Cav, who reluctantly agreed.

The two men walked down the long passageway and back towards the flight hangar.

Cav probed Kryton for more information, who appeared reluctant to share more at first. The 'need-to-know' principle was well ingrained in the intelligence professional.

Cav grabbed his friend by the shoulder and turned to him. The look in his eyes was serious but sincere.

"My head hurts like hell and I'm not sure I'll hear much for a while. Be straight with me, eh!"

Kryton looked at his friend. If he couldn't trust Cav, he couldn't trust anyone.

"It looks like it's a rogue element who the Americans suspect to be one of their own. I'm off to Taipei to chase him down."

Cav's head dropped.

"Wow. I suppose that lets the Chinese off of the hook then?"

"We're not sure yet, but it seems unlikely it was them. Our encounter on the island suggests that they aren't directly involved," said Kryton.

"But how did they find their sub? Perhaps they're trying to cover their tracks?" suggested Cav.

"Maybe. That's what I have to go and find out."

The two men continued walking into the flight hangar. The large door leading to the flight deck was open. The setting sun delivered a beautiful red and orange glow that illuminated the sky. A soft sea breeze filled the hangar.

"Need me to come?" asked Cav hopefully.

Kryton looked over to where the rest of the team were lying stretched out on a row of green footlockers, getting rest after their intense few days.

"Sorry mate, this one's just me. You'd better go and get some rest."

18

Kryton sat up suddenly in the bed, startled by the loud knock on the door of his hotel room. He looked down at the clock on the bedside table. The red LED lights told him that it was early evening. A flatscreen television silently displayed an American news broadcast on the wall at the end of the bed.

The knock on the door occurred again.

"I'm coming," he shouted through a stifled yawn.

He jumped out of bed and walked towards the door. He wore a pair of black tracksuit pants but didn't bother putting on a top. He held his Sig Sauer pistol tightly in his left hand as he looked through the peephole.

"Library service, sir," said the diminutive Taiwanese man on the other side, well dressed in a neat grey three-piece suit; coat, vest, slacks and silk tie over a white shirt – the standard uniform of the concierge of the hotel.

"I asked for a DVD," replied Kryton.

"I think you'll prefer a book, it's more educational," came the reply.

To the outsider, it may have appeared a rather disinteresting conversation, but it was all for a reason.

It was a coded conversation.

The initial innocuous phrase was designed to elicit a specific response, while the response was designed to elicit the third phrase which ensured that the two men who had never met each other before could adequately confirm the other's identity.

Kryton kicked out the small wooden wedge he had placed under the door preventing people from being able to get in. He opened it slightly, and looked down at the Taiwanese man who wore a beaming smile. The man passed him a small box and walked off without saying another word.

"Thank you," said Kryton softly before closing the door and replacing the wedge.

He returned to the bed and sat on the edge of it. The small parcel was wrapped in brown paper. He unwrapped it, uncovering a small cardboard box. He opened it up.

The CIA had agents everywhere. Many were given simple tasks, unaware of what their actual purpose was. Like handing a plain brown package to a stranger.

Inside was a small radio receiver with an earpiece and an electronic tablet. Kryton knew exactly what it was. His orders.

He powered up the tablet and entered a previously arranged codeword. This activated the connection to the encrypted satellite hovering in the atmosphere above. He placed the tablet back on the table and waited.

He walked over to the window and opened the curtain. Several lines of water streaked down the exterior from where the intermittent rain had been falling. It was the first time he had looked outside since his commercial flight had landed from Manila and he had set himself up in his room on the fourteenth floor eight hours earlier.

He had slept like a baby ever since, waiting on further instructions, which would soon come through via the tablet.

Meanwhile, nearly three-thousand kilometres away on Guam, the combined CIA-ASIS team were busy at their improvised operations centre in the SOCCE. A small-signal beeped on a computer.

"Jonas, package delivered," said a young female analyst to the Australian spy running the centre.

Jonas walked over, still tired from his own flight over from Australia.

"Have we got the location of the phone for 'X-ray One'?" he asked, referring to the phone that Wallis had been communicating to in Taipei.

"Yes."

"Okay. Send it," he said.

With the tap of a button, she completed the link to the tablet sitting in a hotel room in Taipei.

Back in the hotel room, Kryton stood in the bathroom looking at his reflection in the mirror as he washed some water over his face. He looked fatigued and tired.

He was happy to be back in the thick of things, but he wondered if maybe it was a case of being careful what you wish for. The people they were going up against had proven that they were willing and able to kill, and in the game of geopolitical chess, there were always casualties. And they usually came from in his line of work.

It wasn't unusual for the best operators to question their choice of work. Only the insane ones didn't; the sort who were likely to go rogue, to chase personal agendas or act as mercenaries for the highest bidder. They weren't the ones you wanted defending a country.

His thoughts were interrupted by a beep from the tablet sitting out on the table.

Kryton walked over and picked it up. The encrypted instructions told him that they were tracking the phone that Wallis had likely been talking to and that it was actually nearby and active. They had a phone, but not a person to go with it. His role would be to get in close and to identify the person with it. If possible, he would also try to gain any covert imagery.

From there, an in-country surveillance team, working for the CIA but made up of local personnel, would be guided to the target to follow the person or persons in order to gain more information.

The aim was to build a complete intelligence picture. To find out who was behind the attack, who had funded it, and more importantly of all, what they might be going to do next.

He smiled.

Amazing technology we have, he thought to himself, impressed at how his cyber and signals intelligence counterparts had been able to locate a tiny little phone and track it halfway across the world.

But technology wasn't enough. Nothing could replace actual eyes and ears on the ground. That's where Kryton came in. His skills allowed him to get close to high-risk targets, to blend into his environment and gain access and information that was unable to be gained by other means. Taipei was a modern city and had many western tourists. He would be able to keep a relatively low profile.

He quickly changed into a set of dark denim jeans, a charcoal polo top, and a black leather jacket. He tightened the laces on his black Merrell shoes. He holstered and concealed his pistol under his jacket and attached the radio receiver to the belt near his back pocket. It would be able to piggyback off of the mobile phone towers around the city and up to the encrypted satellite.

Young Taiwanese youths would be planning their night out over their smartphones, gleefully unaware that a major international intelligence operation was being communicated alongside their own messages.

Kryton looked down at the bustling streets below. The heavy clouds made it appear like it was later in the evening, but in reality, it was still only twilight.

He looked up and across at the mammoth Taipei 101 building situated opposite his hotel. A mix of modern western and Asian style architecture, it had at one point been the tallest building in the world.

He placed the earpiece into his ear and activated the receiver.

"Nest – this is Poseidon," he said softly.

In the SOCCE on Guam, Jonas smiled as the communication from Kryton came across the loudspeaker. He wore one of those headphones with the mouthpieces coming out of the side, similar to the ones that all the NASA controllers are seen wearing in astronaut movies.

"Roger, Poseidon – this is Nest. Read you loud and clear."

"Also loud and clear," replied Kryton.

He looked at his reflection in the window.

What a difference a few weeks made. He inhaled deeply and clenched his fists, before simultaneously releasing the air from his lungs and wriggling his fingers in an outstretched motion.

A sly smile appeared on his face. Any doubts had only been momentary. He wouldn't be anywhere else in the world.

19

Kryton walked down the stairs of the main lobby of the hotel. An eclectic mix of businessmen, western tourists, and locals on holiday moved around the large floor space.

"Okay, Jonas, what's the update?" asked Kryton quietly into the microphone securely pinned to the inside of his shirt.

Jonas walked behind a row of computers, looking up at a screen showing a live satellite feed of downtown Taipei. Clouds intermittently passed across the screen, as the powerful cameras tried to penetrate the storm passing overhead.

Next to that was a large electronic map showing the same location. To the south and out front of the hotel was a blue icon indicating Kryton's location. About a mile and a half away to the west near a market district was a red icon. A circular ring pulsated around a small dot in the centre, indicating the anticipated location of the phone, which would be somewhere within the circle.

Depending on the strength of the signal, the ring could be tiny, thus making the phone easy to locate, or it could be large, meaning that in a crowded area it could be much harder to find.

"The weather's going to make it hard to give an exact location," Jonas said into his own microphone, talking directly to Kryton.

"It wouldn't be fun if it was easy," replied Kryton drolly as he walked at a brisk pace towards the target.

One of the female ASIS technicians sitting behind a computer communicated simple instructions across the satellite and into Kryton's ear.

He tried to keep under the cover of the shops and buildings as he moved past the other pedestrians and through the bustling traffic. He knew the weather would be making it hard for the satellite so he wanted to get to the location quickly.

"Where are we with Wallis?" he asked as he moved along the streets.

Jonas sighed.

"We don't know. We've seen no communication from his phone in the last eight hours. The *Delaware* lost the sub in the South China Sea due to the shallowness of the waters. They had to go quiet due to all the Chinese Navy activity in the area."

Kryton closed his eyes and grimaced in disappointment. He understood the difficulties of tracking submarines in hostile waters, but it was frustrating none-the-less.

"Where do you think he is?" he asked as he jumped over a puddle and moved across the road, skilfully evading a taxi and a small bus.

"It's most likely that he was moving to Taiwan, based on the intelligence we have. We're trying to find out what may be of interest to him there," said Jonas, looking down at his team who were busily analysing intelligence coming in from all over the world.

Kryton was now at the famous night markets. It was brimming with people: tourists and locals alike. A market vendor tried to offer Kryton meat of some kind, but he politely declined and kept walking.

"Up the end of the street and left. One-hundred metres," came the soothing voice still giving him directions.

She sounds like that lady who gives the directions on the Google maps, he thought to himself.

He deliberately placed his hand over his jacket to where his pistol was concealed. An old habit confirming his kit was positioned and ready if needed.

He continued walking up the laneway. A myriad of carts and small shops lined the narrow street. Bright lights shone over the entire area, exacerbated by the small puddles on the ground which reflected the illumination.

The distinct odour of stinky tofu, a local delicacy, unappealingly whipped at his nostrils.

He arrived at the end of the street and turned left as directed. Jonas watched on the electronic map as the blue and red icons started to come closer together.

"Ninety-metres. Go to a small entrance of a department store," came the instructions.

Kryton kept walking at a brisk pace. He was starting to wonder how he would find anyone in this crowd. He arrived at the entrance of the food court and looked around. He walked in.

"Go straight, fifty metres and to your right."

"Roger," replied Kryton, moving in the direction as instructed.

108

It was a relatively cool night, but the anticipation and the pace with which he had been moving was making him slowly perspire.

He weaved his way through the tables and chairs. He was now off of the street and inside what appeared to be a group of shops and restaurants. It was like a small shopping mall.

He walked the fifty metres and turned right.

"I'm at the front of a restaurant," Kryton said, scratching his nose while he spoke to mask the movements of his mouth.

"Kryton," said Jonas in a serious tone as he took a step closer towards the screens inside the SOCCE, "X-ray One is inside. We can't get any better accuracy of the location I'm afraid."

Kryton felt a small chill go down his spine.

Okay, where are you? he thought to himself.

He knew that the phone could be in the possession of any one of the numerous people sitting and moving around the restaurant inside. The issue was trying to find the right one. He grabbed a menu from the front counter, seeking to blend in as a customer. He opened the leather folder and held it up to his face, looking over the top of it just enough to allow him to scan the room.

It was a very nice-looking restaurant, serving a mixture of Chinese and Taiwanese delicacies. Several rows of tables were divided down the middle by a large tank filled with lobsters. The decorative castles inside the tank helped give ambience to the place.

Would he be with others?

Would he be alone?

Kryton's thoughts raced rapidly through his mind. He had to make a quick assessment and act decisively.

"Can I help you?" asked a very friendly waitress in accented English.

"Just a table for myself, please," replied Kryton.

He scanned the room again.

"Over to that side, if possible," he said whilst motioning to the right side of the restaurant, seeking to get closer to something that had caught his attention.

"Okay, please come with me," said the diminutive lady who hurried off to a small table by the side of the wall.

Kryton struggled to keep up with her as she expertly moved in between the waiters and customers. She guided him to a table set for two. He sat down while she removed the other set of plates and cutlery. He angled his chair so that he could better see the other customers.

A young waiter instantly came up and poured him a glass of water.

Kryton sipped on in, taking the time to have a better look inside the room.

"I'm seated inside and observing," he said quietly as the glass obscured his mouth.

He covertly scanned the tables nearby.

A group of young girls were giggling as they shared images on their phones. A mother tried to feed her toddler sitting in a high chair who didn't want to eat right now. A group of Japanese businessmen were slowly becoming more raucous as the bottles of Zhujiang brand beer piled up on their banquet table next to him.

It can't be any of them, he thought.

"Kryton, it's transmitting now!" exclaimed Jonas across the radio.

Kryton looked around. He couldn't see anyone on a phone. He opened the menu again and lowered his head.

"Are you sure I'm in the right place?" he asked.

"Affirmative. It's definitely in there somewhere," replied Jonas.

"I might have to move to another –" said Kryton before he cut himself off mid-sentence.

To his left and near the door to the kitchen several tables away, he saw a lone Chinese looking man sitting next to the rear wall and texting on a fancy looking phone. A waiter had been blocking Kryton's view while clearing plates from a nearby table.

"Wait one," he said softly.

About mid-thirties and wearing a black vest with matching slacks, as well as a white shirt, he looked similarly dressed to the waiters in the restaurant.

Kryton knew he wasn't, though. His hair was cut closer and his build was stockier than the wiry waiters with their scrappy 'K-pop' style haircuts. To the untrained eye, he appeared to fit in, but to Kryton he stood out.

Military perhaps? speculated Kryton to himself.

The man had obviously been in the restaurant for a while as he had an empty plate in front of him.

There was no sign that he was waiting for or had company.

"Possible x-ray one identified," Kryton informed the SOCCE.

Kryton pulled his encrypted phone from his pocket and managed to take several quick covert snaps of him through the Japanese men whose loudness was starting to draw unwanted attention in Kryton's direction.

The man continued to fiddle with the phone, his brow was deeply furrowed and he looked highly focused. Kryton was now certain he had his target.

As the man put the phone back into the pocket of his pants, one of the Japanese men knocked over a bottle of beer, causing it to break. The noise and commotion forced the man to look up in Kryton's direction, alarmed as one of the loud Japanese jumped up and back from his chair while laughing, almost falling into the lone Chinese man's table.

The two lone men made eye contact, which they held for just long enough to make the Chinese man notice and take interest in the Australian.

Kryton looked away first, trying to appear disinterested by looking back at his menu.

"He might have clocked me," said Kryton, informing the SOCCE that he was concerned that the man might have been suspicious at Kryton's presence.

"Zach, something's going on. We're getting information through liaisons. You can't lose this guy," replied Jonas.

Kryton turned his head slightly to try and look back at the man through his peripheral vision.

It didn't take an expert in body language to see that the man was now looking nervous. He was fiddling with a glass of water and his nose was twitching.

He moved to get up, placing a previously unseen small black backpack onto his shoulders. He took a few paces towards the entrance before a waiter with a tray full of empty dishes walked through the small path between tables and bumped into the man. This caused some of the plates to drop onto the table with the businessmen, causing several of them to start laughing even louder and two of them to jump out of their seats.

This drew the attention of the entire restaurant. The waiter tried to apologise to the man, drawing his cleaning cloth from his back pocket and trying to wipe some liquid off of the front of his shirt. The man just looked straight over at Kryton's direction.

He grabbed the waiter by the shoulders and forcefully threw him into the table with the businessmen. He ran towards the back of the restaurant and through the door leading into the kitchen.

Kryton launched himself from his seat and gave chase, jumping over a chair that had been knocked over and slamming through the same door the man had just gone through. He looked down at one of the chefs, who was sprawled out on the floor after obviously having been knocked over.

Kryton saw a door near the fridge swinging open. He ran through it and was now in a bin area in a dimly lit back alley.

20

Rain was softly falling, forming small puddles that mirrored the neon lights of the street.

Kryton looked up the alley and saw the man running through another door. He sprinted through the puddles and proceeded through the same door. A frying pan barely missed his head as he entered yet another kitchen. Several young men looked startled as they stood in their chef uniforms, yelling obscenities in Mandarin as Kryton regained his composure and chased the man through the kitchen and into the dining area.

"Chasing this guy now," he said to the SOCCE, making no effort to conceal his voice this time.

"We need him," replied Jonas, offering no other explanation.

You come and bloody chase him then, Kryton thought to himself as he continued after his target.

The man ran out the front of the restaurant and up a set of stairs. Kryton followed, bounding up the stairs two at a time. The two of them sprinted up the side of an empty shopping centre before the man jumped over a railing and onto a garden bed below. Like a parkour expert, Kryton jumped after him, rolling off of the garden bed and onto the marble floor.

He chased him out of a set of sliding doors and into the street.

The man ran up the road, turning right and into the night markets where people were still bustling and shopping, despite the inclement weather.

Kryton continued to give chase, weaving in and out of the vendor carts and jumping across carpets with cheap trinkets laid out on them which the owners were trying to cover with pieces of plastic.

Kryton was surprised by how fast the man was moving, even with the backpack on. He swiped at the curtains hanging from the awnings of the vendor's carts, struggling to keep pace with the man and not lose him in the crowd.

Suddenly, he came to a dead-end in the street, marked by the brick covered side of a larger building. Kryton looked left and right. The left side had a small laneway leading to another back alley, while the right side had a laneway that led to a darkened corner. He was breathing heavily, but still keeping alert.

The rain had stopped, and the echo of thunder could be heard in the distance. Kryton looked down at an elderly security guard sitting on a milk crate and smoking a cigarette. He returned Kryton's gaze, seemingly unperturbed by the sudden appearance of the sweating Caucasian man who was now holding his pistol in his right hand.

"*Ta qu nali?*" said Kryton, using his very limited knowledge of Mandarin to ask 'where is he' whilst gesturing to his back and hoping the guard understood he wanted to know about the man with the backpack.

The guard simply pointed to the lane to the right.

Kryton nodded, then raised his pistol and slowly walked into the lane. His heart was beating heavily, from both the chase and from the anticipation of walking into the unknown.

The poorly lit laneway had many shadows.

As he proceeded up the laneway, Kryton could see that there was only a bunch of bins at the end, as well as some doors which he assumed led back into more shops and restaurants. The doors had some boxes in front of them, indicating that they hadn't been opened for a while. To the right was another doorway.

Kryton drew his pistol close to his chest, which would allow him to turn the corner with as low a profile as possible. He jogged the last few paces until he was at the edge of it. He turned the corner quickly, rapidly extending his arms holding the pistol, ready to engage what he expected to be a target.

Nothing.

It was just a small courtyard with some boxes and bins. Another dead-end.

Shit, Kryton thought to himself, realising he had chased a shadow.

He turned quickly, but was met with the full force of a backpack being cracked across his face. It knocked him onto his backside, forcing him to drop his pistol. His years of martial arts training ensured that he was able to control his fall, and he managed to spread the impact of hitting the wet concrete throughout his body.

He looked up quickly and saw the Chinese man looking back down at him. The man looked to Kryton's left side and saw the pistol a few feet from where the Australian was spread out on the ground.

Kryton reached out for his weapon, but the man stepped forward speedily and kicked it away, sending it spiralling along the ground and under a pallet of wooden crates. He then tried to stomp on Kryton's head, but the experienced fighter manoeuvred his body out of the way.

Kryton spun around on his back, kicking the man in the side of the knee, forcing him to stumble. The man managed to stay on his feet, but it was enough to allow Kryton the time to get back up.

Kryton raised his hands. The two men eyed each other off for a moment. Kryton now stood at the doorway, blocking the man's only escape. He also raised his hands, ready for the fight.

The man lunged at Kryton, striking out with a jab that Kryton easily parried. He then kicked forward with his right foot, forcing Kryton back a step. The man tried to follow up with another front kick, but Kryton quickly stepped in to close the gap between them, kicking at the man's right knee before he could get the full force behind his attempted strike on Kryton.

The counter-move had the desired effect, causing the man to buckle and drop his head forward. Kryton then delivered a devastating uppercut under the man's nose, forcing his head to snap back and his arms to flail aimlessly.

The Australian now had the initiative and executed a follow up with two double punches to the man's sternum and stomach, causing him to make the most gruesome groan as his body started to shut down. Kryton then stepped forward, grasping both of the man's ears and pulling his head down. He drove his right knee directly into the man's nose, making an audible crack that could probably be heard in the next street.

Blood started pouring down the man's face from his shattered nostrils.

Kryton wasn't finished yet. He twisted the man's head, naturally forcing his body to turn with it as the neck struggled to keep his body aligned. The Australian extended his arm around the man's neck, while his other arm simultaneously reached behind the man's head to lock him in a rear-naked choke.

Kryton dropped to one knee and squeezed. The man tried to squirm violently, but the pressure was too tight.

His nose broken, blood pouring from his face and his internal organs battered, the man didn't hold up for long. In a few seconds, the gurgled groaning stopped as the man passed out. Kryton released the grip, not wanting to kill him. He gently placed the man's head down onto the ground.

Kryton stood up and ran over to retrieve his pistol. He then moved to where he had been knocked over a few moments earlier and retrieved the radio receiver that had fallen off of his belt.

"Nest, Nest – this is Poseidon. Do you hear me?" he asked as he fiddled with his earpiece.

"We have you," replied Jonas. "What the hell's been going on?"

Kryton looked over to where the man was lying flat on the ground. He ran his hand over his own face, a dull pain finally starting to set in from where he had been smashed by the backpack. He checked his teeth.

All were still intact, much to Kryton's relief.

"I've caught up with the guy, we got into a bit of a stoush," Kryton informed the SOCCE.

"Is he still alive?" asked Jonas, knowing what Kryton was capable of.

"Yeah, but he's out of it for now."

Kryton ran over to the man and rifled through his pockets, pulling out the mobile phone he had been playing with in the restaurant.

"Kryton, we're getting told that there is a secret meeting between Chinese and Taiwanese authorities tonight to discuss everything happening. Apparently, they're trying to find a diplomatic solution. It's under the cover of a business cocktail party."

"Let me guess, at the 101 building," said Kryton.

"Yeah. How did you know?" asked Jonas curiously.

Kryton looked down at the electronic identification key card he had just pulled from the man's vest pocket. It had both Mandarin and English writing on it, as well as a picture of the man. The logo at the top clearly indicated it was for the Taipei 101 building. Kryton observed the writing in English.

'Hospitality staff' it said across the bottom.

"This guy has an access card to the 101. It looks pretty legitimate."

Kryton thought for a moment under the dull light of the secluded courtyard. The loud crack of thunder indicated that another storm was approaching.

"Anything else?" asked Jonas.

Kryton looked around the area, and remembered the backpack that had left his face hurting. He ran over to where it was and opened it up. He pulled out the contents inside.

His jaw dropped.

"Oh, shit," he whispered.

"What is it?" asked Jonas.

Kryton didn't answer straight away. He looked at the man's phone and scrolled through the recent messages. The last text, obviously received when he was at the restaurant based on the time next to the message, was short but foreboding.

'It's going ahead. 60 minutes. Meet at kitchen,' it simply read.

Foreboding because Kryton had found several bricks of plastic explosive, as well as a timer with a detonator, in the backpack.

He jumped up and started sprinting.

"Zach – what is it?" asked Jonas again.

Kryton stopped to put the backpack into one of the bins. They could come and retrieve it later.

He continued out the way he came and aimed for the street.

"Jonas, I found a bag with C4 explosives and a timer. I think they're going to attack that meeting. You've got to stop it going ahead," he exclaimed.

Jonas' eyes widened as the other analysts turned their heads in shock to look at his reaction. The lead CIA representative jumped up from her seat and went over to have an intensive conversation with him.

They spoke for a few moments.

"Jonas, talk to me," said Kryton as he ran into the main street and towards his target.

"We can't do anything until we know for sure what is going on," said Jonas matter-of-factly. "We were informed about this through a deep cover source. We can't risk blowing their cover by announcing our knowledge of the meeting. Besides, we need to find out who is there."

Kryton knew Jonas was right. This was the job, taking risks in highly complex and dangerous situations.

Kryton could see the Taipei 101 building up ahead, towering over the city. A dull blue light shone from the pinnacle at the top like a candle. He estimated it would take him five minutes to cover the distance on foot. A sharp bolt of forked lightning illuminated the sky, quickly followed by a deafening crack of thunder.

Kryton looked down at his watch and tried to do some mental arithmetic. He figured that it had been forty-five minutes since the text had been received. That gave him less than fifteen minutes to get to the building, find the meeting and try to stop a likely attack.

Kryton kept running. He was glad that he had kept at least some of his cardio up even after having to leave the army, even if the island walk had been harder than he would have liked.

Just over five minutes later, he reached the front of the huge structure. It appeared very busy inside, holding a mix of residential and commercial interests that drew people from all over the world. The foyer had a beautiful marble design with large palm trees adding to the aesthetics. Despite being a decade old, it still looked and smelled brand new.

Kryton exhaled, before drawing in air deeply to get his heart rate down.

He looked around, trying to find the elevators. He found them.

"I'm in the building," he said to the SOCCE.

"Mate, if this meeting gets attacked, it could look like it was revenge for the Air Force One attack or independence activists. Either one could provoke the situation. You've got to stop it and find out who is behind it. This might be our best chance," said Jonas.

Kryton found a digitised information board. It had the entire building structure on it, showing each level and the contents within. He scrolled his finger up from the base. On the 50th floor, he found what he was after.

The function centre level. If they were going to hold a meeting with hospitality staff, that's where it would be.

He looked back to the base of the board to find the service elevators. He assumed that if it was such an important and secretive meeting, he wouldn't be able to access the floor via the normal elevators.

Once he identified where they were located, he raced to a door hidden away at the rear of the lobby.

It was locked.

He stood back and looked at it. An electronic keypad was jutting out from the wall next to it. He pulled out the identification card he acquired from the man back at courtyard, swiped it and prayed it would work.

It did.

The door opened, leading to a smaller foyer which contained two elevators with wide doors. He was in the right place.

He pressed the button.

Looking up above the doors, he could see the LED pad displaying the floor numbers as the elevator descended.

30, 29, 28…

Come on, come on, Kryton thought to himself, willing it to descend faster.

14,13,12…

"I'm heading up the service elevator to the function centre. Let's hope I'm in the right spot," he said.

A few moments and what seemed a lifetime later, the elevator opened. He jumped in and pressed the button to the desired floor. He looked down at his watch. He had maybe six or seven minutes until the meeting as per the text from the man's phone.

Fortunately, the Taipei 101 building had the fastest elevators in the world, and in less than thirty seconds the doors opened. Kryton patted his pistol under his jacket once again, just to be sure.

He stepped out into a non-descript lobby. A stocky Chinese man in a suit stepped in front of him. Kryton could see a curled wire leading to an earpiece sticking out of the rear of his suit jacket.

A bodyguard.

He was about the same height as Kryton.

The man said something sharply in Mandarin.

Kryton smiled and held up the identification card in his left hand and slightly to the side of his face at eye height. The bodyguard looked at it for a moment, before looking back at Kryton in a confused manner.

Kryton just shrugged his shoulders while still smiling. With the speed of a seasoned professional, he drove his right palm into the man's throat. This caused the man to go limp, and Kryton followed it with a punch to the stomach. As the bodyguard's head dropped forward, Kryton grabbed the side of it and rammed it with great force into the wall next to the elevator, enough to knock the man out but not do any long term damage.

Kryton held up the unconscious man long enough to drag his body into the open elevator. He pressed a button to a higher floor and stepped out just as the doors closed, taking the bodyguard up towards the roof.

Kryton walked over to a set of double swinging doors. As he got closer, he could hear the clanging of pans and the clinking of glasses. He knew it was the kitchen. He stopped just short of the doors and looked in through the small circular window of one of them. Inside the kitchen were a mix of chefs and waiters, busily preparing canapes and pouring champagne into crystal glasses. The waiters were dressed just like the man Kryton had fought back out on the streets.

"Jonas, I'm at the function centre. What should I be looking for?" he asked the team running the operation on Guam.

Jonas looked around at his team. No one was really sure. They were struggling to isolate the connection to the phone that had sent the text.

"We...we don't know. Try to find another bomb, perhaps."

Kryton mouthed an obscenity to himself. He had made it this far, yet now he wasn't sure what was about to happen. He looked back into the kitchen. Sitting on the inside near the door was a chef's tunic. One of the staff members had obviously removed it or had gone off somewhere else.

Kryton thought for a moment.

If the man he had fought had a bomb and was disguised as a waiter, it was likely he would try to access the main floor with all the VIPs.

Kryton subtly opened the door near the table and grabbed the tunic. He replaced his leather jacket with it, adjusting the holster and radio receiver.

He stepped into the kitchen unnoticed. The smell of fresh seafood wafted throughout the air. Picking up an empty tray, he stood by a set of shelves and looked intensely around the kitchen. It was now past the sixty-minute mark. Out of the corner of his eye, he saw a Caucasian man standing by a kitchen top about fifteen metres away. It appeared odd because almost all of the other staff were ethnically Asian. Kryton ducked down to get a better look through the preparation tables where some of the chefs were working. The man was standing side on, but Kryton could see clearly enough.

"Jonas," said Kryton into his radio, "Wallis is here."

The Australian spy on Guam gasped. He composed himself and barked an instruction to his staff.

"Get onto the local assets and get Taiwanese law enforcement to that location, right now."

Kryton watched as Wallis looked nervously at his watch. Wallis pulled a phone out of his pocket and tried to make a call. A moment later, a loud ringing noise emanated from Kryton's pocket, audible even above the cacophony coming from within the kitchen.

The Australian dropped the tray and dived into his pocket to pull the phone out, desperately trying to find a button to silence the device. He managed to make it stop, but only after several rings that could be heard above all of the noise.

He looked up worryingly.

Across the room, looking between the shelves and all the kitchen staff, was Wallis staring straight back at him. The American didn't flinch. He simply turned his body slightly and placed the phone down onto the bench, fiddling with something with his other obscured hand.

Kryton went to draw his pistol.

Wallis spun around and extended his right arm. He had already pulled out a pistol of his own and was pointing it straight at Kryton. The Australian sharply turned his body and stepped back.

It wasn't enough. The bullet Wallis fired narrowly grazed his right shoulder. The kitchen staff dispersed in a panic, some diving onto the floor, others running around aimlessly. Kryton dropped to his knees and managed to finally pull out his weapon. People and dishes flew everywhere. Wallis aimed his pistol again, but couldn't get a clear shot. Kryton watched as he effortlessly pushed a waiter to the side and run out of the doors onto the main floor.

He looked down at his shoulder which felt hot. Part of the fabric of the tunic was all torn up and the skin was exposed. A light red line indicated where the bullet had literally scraped across the skin, not causing any real damage.

"I'm in contact with Wallis. He's fled out into the meeting space," said Kryton, starting to give the SOCCE running commentary so that they could hopefully get some support to him.

21

Kryton stood up and pursued Wallis. He jumped over two waiters lying on the floor and pushed through the doors leading to the main floor. It was packed with various important-looking people, all very well dressed who were standing around talking. A table with miniature Taiwanese and Chinese flags was positioned at the top of the room.

It looked like many of the cocktail parties he had attended during his former career working for ASIS.

Kryton knew enough about the political situation in the region to understand that something significant was going on.

Several people by the door looked confused, obviously having heard the gunshot over the music being played by the string quartet in the corner of the room.

He scanned the floor, searching for Wallis. He saw the tall man struggling to get through the dense crowd. Kryton followed, pushing people aside while trying to keep focus on where Wallis was moving.

He got closer, obviously more agile than the American.

Wallis turned to see Kryton gaining on him.

He looked desperate.

He acted accordingly.

Wallis pointed his pistol into the air and fired two shots in quick succession.

The sound of a woman screaming was followed by the commotion of a crowd starting to panic.

The close personal protection teams, until now concealed amongst the crowd, sprang into action, drawing their own weapons and forming tight circles around their principals – the name given in the security industry for the person or persons they're charged to protect.

People started running in all directions in confusion, falling over each other as they looked for cover.

This was the effect Wallis was looking for, as the panicked crowd made it easier for him to move while seeking an escape. Kryton became held up by a small team of bodyguards as they rushed their principal towards one of the exits.

The Australian weaved his way through the crowd and found himself near a hallway. He ran up it.

Wallis appeared from the corner about twenty metres away and fired two rounds. Kryton took cover in a doorway, then raised his Sig Sauer and fired a shot in return, striking the mahogany wall near Wallis' leg.

He ran after the American, still providing a running commentary to the SOCCE.

He turned the corner, ready to instantly fire a shot if a target presented itself. Instead, he saw a door leading to a stairwell hanging open. Kryton looked down and saw a small splatter of blood. He had obviously managed to even the score. He went charging through the stairwell doorway, finding Wallis limping down the stairs.

He could easily have taken the shot, but he knew that people far higher than him wanted the American alive. Kryton launched himself down the stairs, tackling Wallis and forcing both men to fall to the concrete floor.

Wallis recovered first, now in an elevated position a few steps above the Australian. He looked around for his weapon which he had dropped. Kryton moved up two of the steps to close the gap, punching Wallis in the left rib, causing the man to buckle. He followed up with a left hook, which was expertly blocked by Wallis. It was obvious that the former NSA agent had some skills.

The American countered with a body shot to Kryton's stomach, forcing him back down the stairs, making him wince. The adrenalin masked the pain, and Kryton once again moved up the stairs, grabbing Wallis by the leg as he tried to run back up to the stairwell. Wallis kicked out with his other leg, which Kryton managed to parry with his free hand.

Kryton attempted to grab Wallis by the shoulder but was met with an elbow to the face, once again knocking him back down the stairs and onto the concrete floor.

Kryton came to a halt in the corner of the stairwell, next to a water pipe. Stars filled his vision, and he felt the warm trickle of blood running down into his mouth. He thought for a moment that Wallis had broken his nose.

It certainly wouldn't be the first time that had happened to him.

Kryton shook his head to try and clear his vision. He looked up and saw Wallis, who had obviously recovered, raise the pistol straight at his head.

Kryton's heart skipped a beat. His own pistol was sitting at his feet. It might as well have been on the moon. He looked straight back at Wallis. There was not a thing he could do.

"You should have shot me," said the American simply with a slight grin.

Kryton steeled himself for the end.

A sharp spark shot out from the water pipe above Wallis' head. The American flinched, before looking up to the stairwell above. His eyes widened. He moved quickly to his right, before raising his pistol and firing two shots up towards someone Kryton couldn't see from where he was sprawled out.

Kryton reached forward to his feet, picked his own pistol up and pointed it at Wallis' direction. The American had opened the door and fled back out to the function centre main floor.

Kryton tried to stand up, but a sharp, debilitating pain shot through his leg.

Fucking knees, he thought to himself. The fall from where Wallis had knocked him had triggered an old parachuting injury. Despite all that was going on, Kryton was able to see the irony of how the injury that had forced him out of the army in the first place was now rearing its ugly head.

He slowly managed to get to his knees, trying to communicate with the SOCCE.

Nothing.

The stairwell seemed to be playing havoc with his communications.

He watched as a pair of legs slowly made their way down the stairs above him. He raised his pistol, not knowing what to expect. He watched as a Chinese lady softly walked down onto the stairwell on the level above. She had a pistol in her right hand. She placed her left hand to her ear and said something in Mandarin – obviously having better luck with her communications equipment.

She looked down at Kryton. He lowered his pistol, keeping his finger on the trigger just in case. She raised her hands by her side, a gesture to show she was no threat.

Kryton sat in the corner, breathing heavily. Pain was ravaging his body. It had been a long time since someone had got the better of him like that. He watched as she slowly descended the stairs. She was in her early thirties, wearing a dark pantsuit with her shoulder-length black hair tied into a ponytail.

When she reached the bottom of the stairs, she knelt down and looked at Kryton. She smiled, looking over his body to check for any significant damage.

Kryton looked at her, unsure of what to say.

She spoke first, in perfect, soothing English.

"I'm Agent Chen of the Ministry of State Security. You must be Zach Kryton."

Zach Kryton will be back…

Please feel free to follow us on social media and provide recommendations and feedback!

INSTAGRAM

joshfrancis_red.diamond

FACEBOOK

joshfrancisbooks

INSTAGRAM

FACEBOOK

AMAZON

Please leave an honest review on Amazon. This helps to tailor better content and allows for reader interaction.

Sign up to the readers group

Biography

Josh Francis qualified as high school teacher before commissioning into the Royal Australian Navy as a junior officer soon after the September 11 attacks in the U.S. A desire to serve on warlike operations saw him resign his commission and enlist into the Australian Army. After qualifying as an infantryman and paratrooper, Josh deployed on peacekeeping operations in Timor-Leste conducting counter-militia operations.

After completing basic and specialist intelligence operations training, Josh completed multiple deployments to Afghanistan and Iraq, conducting duties in conventional and special operations, as well as training roles.

He is the author of the military themed personal development books *The Camouflage Series*, as well as the *Zach Kryton* series of books.